Naomi Shihab Nye

The Turtle of Oman

a novel

ILLUSTRATIONS BY Betsy Peterschmidt

GREENWILLOW BOOKS
An Imprint of HarperCollins*Publishers*

For my wonderful editor, Virginia Duncan, and 20 + happy years of working together.

Always remembering Aziz and the love he shared. To everyone at The American International

School of Muscat—thanks for making a little throne for your guest, and for passing the date plate.

And an ongoing "Mahalo" to Frank Stewart of Honolulu, who changed our lives forever.

The Turtle of Oman

Text copyright © 2014 by Naomi Shihab Nye.

Illustrations copyright © 2014 by Betsy Peterschmidt.

The text of this book is set in 22-point ITC Espirit.

Book design by Paul Zakris

Library of Congress Cataloging-in-Publication Data

Nye, Naomi Shihab.

The turtle of Oman : a novel / by Naomi Shihab Nye.

"Greenwillow Books."

pages cm

Summary: When Aref, a third-grader who lives in Muscat, Oman, refuses to pack his suitcase and prepare to move to Michigan, his mother asks for help from his grandfather, his Sidi, who takes Aref around the country, storing up memories he can carry with him to a new home.

ISBN 978-0-06-201972-1 (hardback)

[1. Emigration and immigration—Fiction. 2. Moving, Household—Fiction.

3. Grandfathers—Fiction. 4. Oman—Fiction.] I. Title.

PZ7.N976Tur 2014 [Fic]—dc23   2014018263

14 15 16 17 18 CG/RRDH 10 9 8 7 6 5 4 3 2 1

First Edition

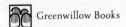 Greenwillow Books

"The flowers of the garden
guide us with their smiles."

SIDI ABOU MADYAN (TWELFTH CENTURY)

Note: Sidi is pronounced "See-Dee."

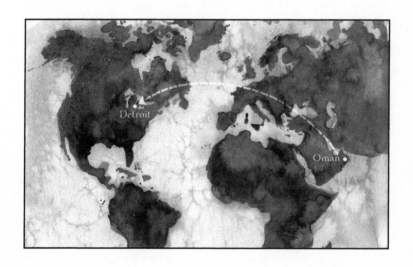

Earplugs

 Aref Al-Amri stared at the Muscat International Airport security guards. They looked very serious in their brown uniforms, checking tickets, waving travelers forward. He was standing with his parents. His dad hadn't stepped into the security line yet. Aref wished he had planned to give his dad a tiny turtle to carry in his pocket. A turtle might hide his head and pretend to be a stone when the plane took off, then stick his head out of the shell again when the plane was flying. His dad could feed him a piece of lettuce from his sandwich.

The airport lobby swirled with people wearing bright scarves, hats and turbans. They pushed baggage carts and dragged trunks and suitcases behind them. Who were they, where were they going, and why? Some people seemed anxious or worried, clumping together with family members, trying to keep track of belongings. Others looked bouncy and chatty. Aref's own mom, standing next to him, attempted to answer her phone in the middle of all that noise. She resembled a tourist from Bahrain.

"Dad," he said, "look how big their suit-cases are."

"Even bigger than yours." Aref's father shook his head. "People want to take everything with them. So loaded down!"

Aref's father had checked a large blue suitcase. He'd been urging Aref to get rid of extra possessions for weeks now, so Aref wouldn't try to pack too much. But Aref didn't like letting go of his things. It was hard to decide. A baby shrieked. Aref shook his head. His mom covered her ear that wasn't on the phone.

"See you soon! Take care of your mom and Sidi and Mish-Mish," said his dad, rumpling Aref's thick hair. "Don't forget to keep speaking English, so you'll be all warmed up. I'm glad you didn't get a haircut. Good choice."

Aref smiled. He didn't even like letting go of his hair. Speaking English was easy, though—everyone spoke it at his American international school and he'd spoken it since he started talking, along with Arabic. It felt natural to speak both. His mom was an English professor at the university, so his family spoke more English than most people. His dad taught biology, so they liked talking about science too. They'd all spoken mostly English at home since his parents had decided to go to the United States. These days, they mostly talked to other people in Arabic—their neighbors, and Sidi, people in restaurants and stores. And they dreamed in Arabic too.

Aref's Dad was wearing a crisp new yellow-and-white checkered shirt and a dark blue jacket with bulging pockets. "What's in your pockets?" Aref asked, patting one. "They're huge!"

"Well, my passport, I hope!" his dad said.

"And my ticket and boarding passes and gum and mints and money and earplugs and my telephone . . ."

"Earplugs?" asked Aref.

"Well, you know . . . sometimes people talk too much," his dad said. "Or I might be sitting next to that baby. What if he gets the hiccups after crying so hard? If the person next to me is old enough to speak, we'll visit a bit before everybody starts to snore. Also, jet engines make a loud roar. I'll need some good sleep before starting my new life. Ask Mom to get you earplugs too."

Aref's mom handed his dad her telephone. "*Maasalameh, shukrun, yallah, alif shukrun iktheer ya ammi,*" he said loudly, over the din.

Then he handed the phone back. "We're not saying good-bye to each other," he said, pointing to Aref and himself. "We're just say-ing, 'See you in a week.'"

"If anyone else calls, I'm not answering," said Aref's mom.

"Sitting next to that baby would be extremely bad," said Aref.

His dad leaned over and whispered in Arabic, "Do you know that someone tried to smuggle a parrot onto a plane last week?"

"Why?"

His dad shrugged. "It's a mystery." Then he glanced at his watch. "It would be strange to be arrested because of a parrot. Well, I won't have to look far at all to be learning something every moment." He smiled at Aref and Aref's mom. "By the time you arrive, I'll have a long list of discoveries."

"I believe you, Dad," said Aref, standing

on one foot like a pelican or a stork. "For sure, you always win."

Discovering Something New Every Day was an Al-Amri family motto. Aref's father said people started playing this game the day they were born. That baby was probably just learning how loud his scream could be.

In your notebook, you wrote down new ideas or even scraps of new information. Nothing was too small. Even the definition of a single word qualified. "Magnanimous." (Very, very generous.) "Stupefaction." (Shocking, astonishing.)

Aref's father liked making lists and had a stack of thin black notebooks he'd been keeping over the years with lists on every page. He wrote in Arabic and English, both. He wasn't taking these notebooks to the United States, though—he was only taking a new, blank one. Aref liked making lists too, but used blue and red school notebooks. His mom kept her new discoveries in the computer.

It was a game that never ended. Usually Aref and his parents traded discoveries at the dinner table. Last night his dad had said, "I learned my flight from Muscat to Ann Arbor will take approximately fifteen hours and nine minutes, not counting the time on the ground changing planes."

"That means you will have to eat breakfast, lunch, and dinner in the sky," said Aref.

"And maybe a snack too," said his dad.

Even Sidi, Aref's grandfather, played the game, but without writing things down.

Sometimes Aref copied what he said. Sidi

specialized in geographical information, such as:

Sultanate Facts

1. Oman is the last sultanate on earth besides one other, Brunei Darussalam, that none of us have ever visited.

2. A Sultanate has a sultan as ruler, not a president or a queen or a Pharoah or a Prime Minister.

3. The sultan is the boss. You don't see him very much.

4. One fourth of the people now living in Oman started out in other countries. They came to Oman to work, or to find a safe place to

call home. Some just fell
in love with the country,
and stayed.

Sidi was fascinated by this, because Oman
had really changed during his lifetime. When
he was a boy, there were very few people from
other countries living there.

Aref's discoveries specialized in animals,
his favorite topic.

Turtles Are My Favorite
1. Green sea turtles can
stay underwater for as long
as five hours, without
coming up to the surface once.
2. Their heartbeats slow down
dramatically. Sometimes
green sea turtles have 9

minutes between heartbeats.
You think they are dead,
but they are only floating.
3. A leatherback turtle can
be six and a half feet long.

When Aref had made this discovery, he wondered how scary it would be for a diver swimming in the ocean if a six-foot turtle, big as a man, swam up to him. You would either want to jump out of the water, or ride the turtle. Aref had drawn a picture of a giant turtle and a regular-sized man in his notebook.

4. Did you know a turtle's
shell is called a "carapace"?
5. Land turtles have back-
bones under their shells, sea
turtles do not.

A crackly voice boomed from the speakers. "All passengers for Dubai, please report immediately to gate fourteen. Flight thirty-six to Dubai will be boarding momentarily." This was not his father's plane.

Aref liked the word *Dubai*. "Good-bye, Dubai, good-bye, Dubai . . ." He spun in a circle and skidded.

Then he ran a little ways and slid across the shiny airport floor, as if he were on the snow slope at Ski Dubai, the indoor ski palace where they had traveled when he was five.

"Careful, Aref!" called his mom. "Don't bump into people!"

Ski Dubai was the only time Aref had ever seen snow—fake snow, slick white bumps built into tubes and slopes, under sparkling electric stars. Outside it was 100 degrees, but inside, people were skiing. It seemed very weird. Michigan would be full of snow during the winters.

"It's time for me to go!" Aref's father finally said. He was flying to Kuwait, Frankfurt, New York, then Ann Arbor, Michigan. Time for him to go through security, where Aref and his mom couldn't follow.

Aref's dad leaned over and kissed the top of Aref's head. "Take good care of your mom, promise? Help her get ready? Do everything she says?"

But what if she said something silly?

"Maybe," said Aref.

His dad punched him lightly. Then he hugged him hard. "See you in a week on the other side of the world!" It seemed impossible.

Aref had planned to drop a stone into

his dad's pocket, but now slipped it into his father's hand instead. He wanted his dad to see how unusual it was.

"It's for good luck," said Aref. "Look, it's a little pink on this side, and if you hold it in the sun, it glitters."

Aref's father turned the stone over and smiled. "You are just like your grandpa," he said. "I will hold it up in the window when the sun rises over the ocean. I will keep it in my pocket always when I arrive in the United States. I will say my son gave it to me, and you are coming soon."

Lemon

Aref and his mother waved and waved until they couldn't see Aref's father anymore.

Aref's mother sighed. "There he goes! Now it's time for you to get packing! Your big green suitcase needs attention!" She reached for Aref's hand. "You could get lost in here. You could be in India before you know it."

They didn't always hold hands like this

anymore. But today Aref squeezed her hand tightly. They walked past a newspaper and gift shop featuring a table of small brown camels. Aref stopped to press the belly of a camel and it made a bleating sound. He pressed it again. A man from India or Kathmandu in an orange robe smiled at him.

"Mom," said Aref, "I wish we were going to India for a vacation instead of Michigan, then just coming home." Many of Aref's good friends at school were from India. He knew about the massive elephants and tigers in the parks and the monkeys that sneaked in through open windows and lifted the lids of pots to see what was cooking. Once his friend Jaz found a monkey on his auntie's kitchen counter scooping up rice with its paw. Aref wished a monkey would sneak in through his window and do his homework. He would make friends with it. He would name it Brother.

Boom! He bumped into a giant red suitcase being hauled by a sparkly diamond lady in super-tall shoes. "*Mint-essif!*" he said. "Sorry!" She frowned and kept on walking.

His mom led him through the door toward the parking lot, chanting, "See you again next week, airport!"

Aref shivered. He didn't want to come back here. He did not want to move to Michigan.

They stood in the blazing parking lot for a moment, staring toward the runways behind the airport. They could see airplanes marked Air India Express, Turkish Airways, and the giant shiny Lufthansa, which was his dad's airplane. They would have stayed to watch him take off, but his plane wasn't leaving for an hour and a half yet, and the parking lot was more than one hundred degrees with no shade.

In the car on the way home, his mom asked, "Where did you get that rock you gave Dad?"

Aref didn't want to say, *I dug it up in the far corner of our yard, past the chairs and table, from between the roots of the fig tree.* He knew his mom didn't like it when he dug too close to roots. How had he known the rock was buried there? Sometimes he just obeyed his shovel and it told him where to dig. It was like a secret magnet to the treasures in the earth.

"I don't know," said Aref quietly. "But it was a good one." He stared out the window. Gazing left up the boulevard crowded with cars and buses, Aref could see the Hajar Mountains, which meant "Stone Mountains," standing behind the low white buildings of the city. Everyone loved those brown mountains that loomed like a comforting wall. He slumped against the backseat and felt like crying.

To the right, palm trees bowed over the road. They swayed and shifted their drying palm skirts. The giant turquoise Arabian Sea had been there every day of his life. He had always known it. Oman was his only, number one, super-duper, authentic, absolutely personal place.

Aref knew how people moved, crossing a street, how they wrapped their scarves, how the call to prayer echoed across the city and made everyone feel peaceful and proud inside. He liked the way large white boulders were stacked beside the water. He even loved the clicking sounds of shoes and animal hooves on the old cobbled streets in the marketplace, called the *souk*. The buzzing and hammering from smoky shops and garages. He loved when shopkeepers who knew his family called to him, "*Marhaba*, Aref! *Tylee shouf*! Come see what we have today!"

At the Souk
1. You can stack fresh apricots like a mountain.
2. Some stores sell Kitchen matches in big boxes with smiling cat pictures on them.
3. You can buy tiny red metal double-decker bus toys from England with doors that really open and spinny wheels.

His father liked a grizzled man named Abu Aziz at an ancient corner shop. He sold clay and brass incense burners for chunks of frankincense and walking sticks with silver knob handles. His stall smelled delicious. An old donkey with sleepy eyes stood tied up outside. Once Abu Aziz had handed Aref a carrot to feed the donkey, who took it sleepily between his teeth and crunched, and ever since then, the donkey had remembered him.

But would it remember him if he were gone for three years?

In Oman, hotels by the sea glittered at night. Aref had watched some of those hotels being built. So he felt like he owned them. When he was younger, he and his grandfather, Sidi, had walked inside the gleaming lobbies and watched people pushing elevator buttons. He had tugged at his grandfather to ride the elevators with him, and sometimes they rode to different floors and walked up and down the halls as if they were staying there. Once they joined a wedding party in a ballroom when the doorman thought they knew the people inside!

In Oman, Aref knew the bulldozers and the birds.

Three birds We See a Lot at the Beach
1. Storm petrels = Smallest seabirds. They look like bats when they fly. They pick out crustaceans and tiny fish out of the waves while hovering.
2. Cormorants = seabirds that eat fish

3. Frigate birds = they cannot walk or swim. Sometimes they fly for a whole WEEK without landing. The males have inflatable throat pouches and their wings make a big W when they fly.

He loved the brightly colored school supply shop for paper and pencils and pens and folders. He knew the exact bin his purple pencil sharpener had come from. He liked Sami at the tennis shoe store who gave him extra shoelaces and Miriam at the dentist's office who always offered him a new toothbrush. He knew the smooth white sidewalk at the Muttrah corniche that his parents said he had taken his first steps on.

Aref leaned forward so he could see his favorite blue billboard shaped like a boat coming up. *Yallah!* it said in Arabic. Quickly! It was for a restaurant called *MARHABA* that served crispy fish in blue plastic baskets. The fish was so tasty Aref always ate it with his fingers, not a fork. And his mom always said, "Don't gobble." Aref had been keeping his eye on that same sign for years now. It meant they were almost home. How would it survive without him? And how could he say good-bye to a restaurant named "Hello"?

Aref's mother turned the steering wheel, circling a speedy roundabout brimming with pink flowers and tall iron lampposts. Cars whizzed past them. They turned at the shining silver water tower with sunlight gleaming on its head. Aref thought Muscat was surely the greatest place in the world.

"Is there any chance"—Aref leaned forward again, speaking in a weird, high voice like a cartoon—"Dad won't like it in America and he will fly home instead? And we won't have to move?"

His mom laughed. "No chance! We've been planning this adventure for years, *habibti*— you know that. You'll be excited too when you see your wonderful school in Michigan and meet your new friends and teachers. After only one day of strangeness, it will feel like home to you. I promise. Think of Dad flying all that way by himself just to get our apartment ready for us—you and I still have so much to do here! We have a whole week of good-byes ahead of us. I have one lecture to give at school and we must sort, pack and get everything cleaned up before we leave. Let's be in a good mood, yes?"

No. It sounded horrible.

His parents would be attending a university in Michigan. They would be called "Doctors" when they came home.

Different Doctors
1. They are not doctors for sick people.
2. They will still be professors at the university in Muscat when they come back, just smarter ones called Doctors.
3. Aren't they smart enough? Why do they need to be smarter?

It made no sense to him. The inside of his head felt like a lemon, squeezed and sour. Someone honked—an orange taxi veered in front of their car. His mother pressed hard on the brake. "What bad driving!" she said.

"But why, Mom? Why do we have to move somewhere? We won't know where anything is. They might not let me play soccer there."

"Aref, we talked about this one hundred times."

"I still don't understand. I won't have any friends."

"Your new friends are waiting for you. They may not know this yet, but they are."

The lemon squeezed and puckered.

"*Anyone* should be excited to travel to another country and have great adventures," Aref's mom said.

"How do you know?"

"Don't forget," she continued, "you do get to come home in three short years. Sometimes when people leave their countries, they are not returning. That would be so much harder, yes? Think of the refugees we know—their homes or villages were wrecked or ruined, sometimes they have to escape their countries without any suitcases at all. With nothing. They have to be very brave, knowing they might never go back. They are much more brave than we have to be."

Aref was sure this was true. His friend Jad was a refugee from the Sudan. His friend Assef was a refugee from Iraq. Many students at the university were refugees. Refugees had to be the bravest people in the world. But he wasn't one, and he didn't know as much as they knew.

Good-bye, Turquoise and Limestone

Aref and his mom drove up the driveway. Their two-story house in a modern new neighborhood was as yellow as butter. They were the first people who had ever lived in it. All of the white and yellow and brownish houses on their street sat peacefully in the afternoon sunlight. No one else was moving away.

"But, Mom," said Aref, "see, I really like this driveway."

She laughed, as if that meant nothing at all.

The driveway was long, smooth and slanted, so the car tilted up to their house, which sat on a sandy hill. Tufts of green and golden grasses grew up in neat, tall bunches along the sides of the house. They looked like ponytails on his friend Sulima's head. Red granite paving stones led from the driveway to the front step. Aref jumped from one stone to another. "*Yallah*, Mom, remember when I couldn't even do this?"

What if he forgot everything he had already learned, by leaving? Three years of being gone were not short. Not short at all. Anything could happen.

Aref raced ahead to their heavy yellow metal front door and slapped it. He knew the strong click the handle made when his mother turned the key. The inside of their house was a deep breath welcoming them back—so quiet, so cool. He knew the long golden sofas, the blue rugs with swirling red edges, the coffee table, the bookshelves. A string of golden bells hung from one wall. He had rattled them all his life. He knew the small orange tree in the corner of the dining room that was laden with bitter tiny oranges you weren't really supposed to eat. Sometimes he broke one in half and placed it open-faced on the patio so birds could nibble it.

Mish-Mish, which meant "apricot," ran up to them meowing loudly the moment they entered the house. Aref knew what his large orange cat wanted. He left his shoes at the front door, went to the kitchen and found the shiny silver sack she loved best. He placed three star-shaped cat treats on top of the food in her bowl and watched her crunch them with her teeth. He leaned over and rumpled her fur and stroked the place that looked like a striped sunset on her chest. He said, "Oh, Mish, I can't stand it." She waved her fluffy tail. What would she think when they just disappeared?

Aref ran upstairs to his bedroom.

"I will miss my school too much!" he shouted to no one, staring at the blue and red soccer ribbons dangling from his bulletin board. He loved his school. It was the only school he had ever known.

Now he would have to go to a new school in Michigan called Martin Luther King, Jr. Elementary. His parents said the school had a space camp. It had International Night, where all the students from different countries shared food and songs. On the website you could see its hallways marked with street signs—Courtesy Avenue, Kindness Boulevard.

A few months ago, his mom had ordered Aref a biography of Martin Luther King, Jr. They read some of the book out loud together, discussing it.

An American Hero
1. Martin Luther King, Jr. jumped out a second-story window when his grandmother died.
2. He was very smart and popular in school. At first he didn't study too hard, but later he became a better student.

33

3. Martin Luther King, Jr. believed in all people being brothers and sisters. He stood up for other people's rights and led marches for freedom.

4. His father, who was also named Martin Luther King, spoke against racial prejudice too.

The doorbell rang, *bing bong*! Aref jumped up from his bed and raced downstairs to answer it. His mom stepped into the living room looking curious.

Diram, his best friend, was standing on the stoop holding a folded white T-shirt, his own mother behind him. The two moms hugged.

Diram laughed as he always did, with three short bursts, "Ha! Ha! Ha!"

He held up the T-shirt. Their photos were on it, with blue stars floating around their heads. Aref took it with surprise and turned to show it to his mom. "Look!" he said. He had never seen school pictures printed on a T-shirt before.

"Now you can't forget me!" said Diram. Aref's mother waved them in toward the living room, but Diram's mother shook her head and said, "Sorry, we can only stay one minute, we have to pick the twins up at ballet."

Diram dodged into the house right under his mother's outstretched arm anyway. He ran up the stairs to Aref's room, Aref following right behind him, and stopped short at the doorway.

"Aref! I am going to miss your room!" said Diram.

"I am too!" They had had so much fun in this room together, making tents with blankets, camping out on the floor, dumping the tub of Legos to build new, tall cities. . . .

"Wait, I have something for you too," said Aref. He gulped. This was going to be hard, but he wanted to do it. He slid open his rock collection drawer and took out the turquoise stone sitting by itself in its folded paper box. Diram loved this stone best. Aref held it out to him. "Here, keep it."

"*Walla!* Are you sure?" asked Diram. "But you love this one!"

"I know," said Aref. "But you love it too. Take it."

Diram clutched it in both his hands,

smashing the paper a bit, and ran down the stairs to show his mom.

Aref followed.

"Look what Aref gave me!" Diram said, holding it up.

Both moms smiled. "Nice!" said Diram's mother.

"I will keep it on my desk," Diram said.

Aref was already missing it a little bit, but he smiled. "Great!"

Diram and Aref had been best friends since kindergarten and now they would not be together. They were the two best soccer players. Diram was the stronger player, scoring the most goals. Aref was second best. He didn't mind. He had less pressure. They even had fun when they lost. Then they would talk about the game, figuring out what to do better next time. They both loved other sports too and hoped to play more of them.

"So, don't forget me, okay?" said Diram.

"I won't forget you," said Aref. "Will you forget me?"

"No!" said Diram. "We made two shirts. The other one is mine. And . . ." He held up the turquoise stone.

"Wait a minute," Aref's mother said. She dashed to the side of the house, and returned with a clay pot of mint. "Here," she said to Diram's mother. "This is the best mint I ever found so far, it loves Omani heat. For your yard!"

"We will think of you with every leaf," said Diram's mother.

Diram and his mother got back into their

car, waving. Aref stood in the doorway holding his shirt.

"What a nice surprise," his mom said.
She looked at him. "Was that hard? The
turquoise?"

He smiled. "It was hard." He liked that she
knew that.

She went back inside.

Aref sat down on the step for a moment
to think about it all. He was surprised when
another car, a blue one, pulled up before he had
even gone back inside. It was Sulima and her
dad! Aref actually turned and rang his own
doorbell himself, so his mom would come outside again and see them too. *Bing bong!*

Sulima jumped from the backseat of the
car and ran up to him. "Aref! I was worried
you had left already!"

"Only my dad left," he said. "Diram was just here!"

"Muna and Lena too?"

"No, they were at ballet."

"It's like a parade," said Aref's mom, stepping outside. "Hi Sulima!"

Sulima held out two packages, one for each of them, wrapped in yellow tissue. Aref opened his and found a blue box with OMAN painted on the top of it. A darker blue sea wave was scrolled across the bottom. "It's for pencils," Sulima said.

Aref's mother opened her package. Inside was a straw fan woven with pink and turquoise colors. "Remember?" Sulima said. "When I borrowed your fan for the school play and then I lost it? Here's a new one to replace it!"

Aref's mom hugged Sulima. "You are so sweet to remember. I'll take this with me!"

Sulima's father was standing by the car smiling. He used to be a deep-sea diver. "We'll miss you all!" he called, waving.

The thought struck Aref, did he need to give Sulima a stone too?

"Wait here a minute," he said, and he ran upstairs by himself.

Sulima was Aref's best friend of the girls his own age. She liked digging and rocks too. She told Aref she was going to be an architect or the president of a construction company someday. Their fathers taught in the same biology department at the university, but her father specialized in marine biology. She had lived with her parents in the United States for two years before she and Aref ever went to first grade. He had to give her a stone.

She liked the rectangular chunk of pure white limestone that looked like snow.

He pulled it out of his drawer, pausing only a second, and carried it downstairs. He held it out to her. "For you! I'll see enough snow."

She looked amazed. "Thank you, Aref!" she said, clutching it tightly in both hands. "Say hi to the United States for me."

Aref frowned.

"Remember what I told you?" Sulima asked. "The zoos and roller coasters and trains and skating rinks are really fun. The ice cream stores have too many flavors, even more than here. You're lucky!"

Oman had no trains. But Aref didn't feel lucky. "I hope so," he said. "I really like this pencil box, thank you."

Mostly he liked that it said OMAN on it.

"Write to me," said Sulima. "Bye!"

She ran back to the car and hopped in, waving. Her father, who had already said good-bye to Aref's parents more than once, waved from the driver's seat, calling out, *"Maasalameh!"*

Aref's mother put a hand on his shoulder. "You have so many nice friends," she said.

She paused before they stepped back inside. "We still need to say good-bye to the Al-Jundi family," she said, looking down the street at their neighbor's plum-colored house.

Saying good-bye was exhausting.

The Most Important Word in the World

Aref ran upstairs to put his new T-shirt and pencil box into his empty gigantic shiny green suitcase that had been sitting for weeks beside his bed. Its mouth was open. It had three zippered pockets on the outside and four pouches on the inside. The lining of the suitcase was printed with blue crown-shaped emblems, like a scarf or a tablecloth.

A cat would definitely fit inside it. Even two small children would fit inside it. He had picked it out himself at the suitcase store with his parents.

Then he fell onto his bed. "I will always like this bed best!" he yelled. He liked the tall wooden bookshelves in his bedroom, the giant boxes of toys from when he was little pushed into the closet, his room's blue ceiling and the lamp over his bed, so he could reach up and click it on while lying on his pillows. He liked the map of the world taped to the wall. His father had poked a pin with a red head into the state of MICHIGAN.

My New Home
1. Michigan has more lakes and ponds than any other state. It has 64,980 inland lakes and

ponds. Maybe I will fall into one.

2. Ann Arbor's nickname is Tree Town.

3. Mackinac Island, Michigan, has no cars on it. You have to take a horse and buggy, or walk. This seems like Oman in the old days. Also, it is strange since Michigan is famous for car factories.

4. The Grand Hotel on Mackinac Island features the world's longest porch.

Aref's twin cousins, Hani and Shadi, two years younger than he was, would be moving into his bedroom while he was gone. His cousins and aunt and uncle, who'd had a job transfer, were coming from Dubai, where the skyscrapers poked the clouds, to live in Muscat, right after Aref and his mom left. It was perfect timing. Everybody could share. It was disgusting and upsetting, actually.

Hani and Shadi would pull two chairs up to Aref's worktable instead of just one, while Aref was far away, in a room he'd never yet seen. They would sleep in his double bed. They would mess everything up. They would look out the window and hear the call to prayer floating across the valley and that sound would be theirs, not his.

They would listen to the cool hush of the air conditioner through his vent. They would use his drawers. This really upset him. What if they broke the blue porcelain knobs off? He couldn't remember how careful they were.

Aref knew for sure he could not leave his official rock collection, now missing two favorites, given to him for his birthday by his parents years ago, in his drawer. He ran to the kitchen. "Mom, I need tissue. Bubble wrap. Something for packing, hurry." He needed to wrap the rock collection in a special box, tape it shut and hide it under his bed, or on a high shelf in the hall closet where no one would ever look. Chips and chunks of serpentine and diorite, greenstone, basalt, each with its own shape and its story. . . .

"It feels lonesome without your father here already," said his mom, handing him a roll of paper towels and some tissues. "Oh well, we'll see him in a week! What are you doing? Are you packing? Would you like to come peel some carrots and help me? I need a helper right now—set the table, pour the water. . . ."

"I will," said Aref. He was feeling anxious. He dropped the tissues and paper towels onto a chair, picked up the little peeler and a scrubbed carrot from the cutting board, and stared at it.

"Mom, could Hani and Shadi just sleep in the living room?" he asked.

"For three years?"

"Yes."

"You are so silly! You don't mind sharing."

"Well, I really do. I just pretended I liked it, for school. We had to."

Miss Nuha, Aref's teacher, whom everyone loved so much, said the word "sharing" was the most important word in the world. She said if people thought first about sharing,

49

they would always get along and the world could be more balanced—those who had too much could share more with those who didn't have enough. Was this true?

Aref and his classmates made posters to illustrate sharing—painting, drawing or collaging images that popped into their minds. Aref painted green and brown speckled turtles on his poster, sharing a wide, dreamy beach. Turtles shared plankton and water and waves and sand. He had fun painting their shells. Sulima painted a much better picture than his—long lines of friends who looked like people in their real class with their arms around one another. Diram painted bright cars in a parking lot, sharing space.

Aref didn't mind sharing sunflower seeds. He didn't mind sharing a crunchy shrimp or two from his Fisherman's Basket at Zad restaurant or the huge pieces of flat bread at the Turkish House. He didn't mind sharing soccer balls or his mini-car collection, which he kept in a tall metal canister—but his friends had to put them back before they left—or pages from a giant tablet of drawing paper.

It was easy to share when you still had what you needed. When you had enough for yourself. Or when you could get whatever you had shared right back again—like his cars.

"Sweet boy, the kids of Ann Arbor, Michigan, will be sharing their town with you too," said Aref's mom.

"I hate sharing," he said.

"No, you don't." Aref's mom put her hands on his shoulders and stared into his face. "A month from now, all your worries will be gone. You will see how silly this was. You will feel excited every morning, just the way you always do."

Aref buried his face in her side. He wasn't crying. "I don't think so," he said.

Memorize

They ate green beans with chunks of lamb and rice for dinner. Aref pushed his water glass to the right-hand corner of his place mat. He liked a square glass, so it lined up properly. No one noticed that he always did this. He liked his fork and spoon lined up exactly straight with the place mat too. He liked finishing one food—all the green beans, for example—before he started eating the rice. He ate the salad last, like a French person, his mom had told him. He drank water between each course. And he liked to eat very slowly.

His dad's chair was just sitting there empty with the echo of his dad in it. By now his dad was—where? High above the clouds. Dozing on a little airplane pillow with his earplugs in his ears. Aref closed his eyes to imagine this.

What did people eat on airplanes?

Jumbo jet menu
1. Dad says they eat sandwiches.
2. Mom says they eat peanuts.
3. Sometimes airplane waiters serve hummus in sealed cups, with a sack of chips. This is hard to picture. But I hope they give it to me.

4. Maybe the passengers gobble gigantic mounds of cotton candy since they are above the clouds.

After dinner, Aref quietly turned the handle of the front door and stepped outside by himself to memorize what his house looked like under the moon. He needed its shape and shadows. He wanted to press all its details into his brain so nothing would disappear.

It would have been nice to walk around the whole neighborhood, staring at every single other house, tucking all their windows and doors and roofs into his memory too. But he was afraid of foxes. At night foxes wandered through the city, poking their noses into gardens and trashcans for scraps. They had large ears and looked regal and a little scary, sneaking around. Aref had seen them from the roof. But he didn't want to meet one up close.

Still, he wished he had been born a fox.

Fox Facts

1. Foxes have fur between their toes so their feet won't get burned on hot ground.

2. The British School has an Arabian Foxes Hockey Club which Diram is going to join.

3. Foxes are not afraid of the dark. They just wander wherever they want to go when they feel like it. No one puts a leash on them.

Even better than a fox, Aref wished he were the endangered Arabian leopard in the Musandam peninsula. Almost no one ever saw it. So they couldn't tell it what to do. He would not wish to be a crab (caught and eaten) or a spiny crayfish (too spiny) or a bonito.

Aref thought about climbing the stairs to their flat roof, where his parents draped the bed quilts on clotheslines for airing and his father often sat with friends in a circle, especially in winter, eating sunflower seeds and drinking tea. In the daylight, you could see the ocean off in the distance. You could see Jabrin Castle. You could wave at the one-hundred-year-old lady Ummi Salwa in her pink satin robe taking a nap in her long chair on the next roof.

When they came back from the United States, Ummi Salwa would be a hundred and three.

Better or Worse

Aref said to his mom the next morning at breakfast, "I dreamed about a word, it was all lit with spotlights."

The word he had dreamed of was "halcyon." In his mind, it looked like a tipped balloon with the air coming out a pinhole on one side. Sulima was throwing it at him and he opened his hands, but dropped it.

Halcyon meant a period of time that was happy and peaceful. You never heard anyone say it, though. That is what my life in Oman has been so far, he thought. And now it will be all shaken up.

"That's nice, *habibti*," said his mom. She didn't ask him what word it was. She probably thought he dreamed about a simple word like "lucky" or "*mabruk*"—"congratulations" in Arabic. She had no idea how many words he knew.

Aref looked out the window at a streak of orange clouds with a bend in it. The clouds reminded him of an arm with a muscle. At breakfast, he nibbled a cucumber, dipped a carrot into the hummus plate. He stared at his scrambled eggs, taking a few small bites. His mother had mixed some white cheese into the eggs. He didn't think he would ever like eggs. But his mom kept serving them. When he was younger, he ate so slowly, his mom said every day was an "endless breakfast" and she made him get up much earlier than his friends did, just to have time to eat before leaving for school.

"How's your place mat memorization coming?" his mom called, trying to distract him from the plate sitting on it.

"Very bad."

A few weeks ago, Aref's dad had bought him a place mat with a map of the United States on it. Aref was trying to learn the names of the fifty states. He kept mixing up Wisconsin and Minnesota. Mississippi was a river AND a state. It was complicated. He hadn't really stared very hard at the western section of the country yet. It was on the left side of the place mat and he was starting at the right. He liked New York and New Jersey.

"Mom, why is there no Old York or Old Jersey?" Aref asked.

"They are in England," his mom said.

"I wish we were moving to England instead," said Aref.

"Why?"

"It's closer to Oman." But it wasn't really close at all. It only looked a lot closer on a map or a globe.

"Why do you have to go back to school?" he asked one more time.

His mother was looking through a thick stack of papers on the table. She still had to grade them. His father graded papers on the computer, like a modern man, but his mother preferred seeing her students' reports and compositions on real paper.

"Well, I do think we've talked about this one hundred times—please try to remember what we said. It's temporary. We'll have an adventure and when we come home, all our lives will be better."

"My life will be worse," said Aref. "Diram will be a Hockey Fox without me. I don't want to speak English all the time. I don't want to meet new people. I will miss my friends and be too far from Sidi. Mom, can Sidi come over today?"

"Guess what, I already called him," she said. "I told him we need his personal assistance, so he is coming over later this afternoon. Isn't that good?"

"Yes. It's great."

Aref went to his room and wrote in his notebook.

Questions
1. Why can't Sidi come with us?
2. Is my handwriting in both English and Arabic getting better?

Slow

Aref and his grandfather had been looking inside and under things for a long time now, checking out new streets, shops and cafes, finding friends, wandering the beaches. Since Aref was little, they had been making plans:

Someday Soon
1. Yes, we will go to Masirah Island and watch kite surfing!

2. Yes, we will march around Al-Hazem Fort and pretend we are living two hundred years ago!

3. Yes, we will visit Jebel Shams, the highest mountain of our country!

4. Yes, we are always looking hard to find the leaf-toed gecko. Maybe it will sit on our feet.

5. Yes, we will see the "magical light" at Wadi Shab. Sidi says it is a long drive and if we sit down and stare, something inside our eyeballs will start to

shimmer. Sidi says the trees look like they are floating in in the sky.

Even when they weren't doing anything special, Sidi and Aref, Team of Two, pretended they were—yes, we will take all the spices out of the drawer and smell them and throw the old nasty nutmeg away! When Aref was little, Sidi would sit quietly on a bench while Aref ran in circles around him. Sidi would close his eyes and say, "I'm soaking up the light" or, "I'm thinking of what we just did, or what to do next."

Sidi knew the real official names of rocks and stones and said it was because he had always lived in view of the Hajar Mountains. He loved that massive wall of brown rumpled slopes and peaks behind the city. Everyone in Muscat looked at those slopes all their lives. Sidi said he was the sultan only of stones.

And Sidi always had time for Aref, since he was retired now and never wore a watch. He didn't like watches. He said time felt heavy on his wrist. He hated rushing and thought the world was hurrying so much that people were missing all the good parts.

Aref had taught Sidi how to use a computer, but Sidi didn't like it. He said the letters on the screen went too fast and made him dizzy. The wealth of information was overwhelming. He didn't want to know the news from Zanzibar.

Aref's mother stood in the doorway of his bedroom staring at him. He was lying on his bed reading a science magazine about glittering galaxies.

"Is there any news about your suitcase, Aref?" she asked. "You don't seem to be making any progress. Why don't you manage a little packing before Sidi gets here? You need to pack the clothes you love most." She had come upstairs from cleaning out the refrigerator and still had a dishrag in her hand. She wanted the refrigerator to be spotless for his cousins and had crammed everything that was left onto one shelf.

"I don't love any clothes."

He was wearing a blue-and-white striped T-shirt and blue jeans. He plucked at them as if he were swatting them away from his body.

Then he jumped up, did a cartwheel on his carpet and landed perfectly. So he did another one.

Know Your
Michigan Turtles

Mish-Mish had followed Aref's mom upstairs and stood on her hind legs batting at the curtain pull. Sometimes she got a claw snagged and tugged hard to free herself. Aref thought she might be trying to close the draperies. She liked dim light for her four-hour naps. Aref thought Mish-Mish was extremely smart. Often she moved her cat-lips as if she were trying to speak.

"Mom, why can't I put Mish-Mish in my suitcase and punch air holes in the top? Hani and Shadi will not take good care of her. They barely know her. What if she thinks we're never coming back and runs away? What if she goes looking for us, what if she gets lost forever?"

It was possible to imagine all sorts of bad things without working too hard. You could think about centipedes curling and writhing under your bed. One might crawl up the leg of your bed and sting you. Or a tiny shriveled mummy person the size of your hand, standing up on your chest in the dark, sending out light-rays, and growling. You could picture your own head falling off without warning, or your human body growing a tail. You could imagine kids in the United States making fun of your accent or your clothes or the ways you did things.

Aref's mother sighed. "Please? Just for a little while? You pick what you want to take with you. You're old enough! If it fits in your suitcase, you can take it." She had been saying that for weeks.

Aref picked up the tourist brochures and postcards of Michigan his mom and dad had been giving him. They had ordered them through the Internet and printed them in color and by now he had a thick collection— snows and bridges and lakes, boats and cherry trees. The biggest lakes were called the Great Lakes. He had to admit Michigan looked like a very nice state. He stuck the stack of pictures into a suitcase pocket. Then he took them out. If he was moving there, why did he need to pack the pictures? He would see everything in real life soon enough.

On his desk he had placed his favorite brochure of all, *Know Your Michigan Turtles*. When this one arrived, Aref went a little crazy in a happy way.

"How did they know? How did they know I like turtles the best?" he had asked.

His dad had raised one eyebrow and shrugged his shoulders. "Maybe everyone in Michigan likes turtles," he said.

Aref learned that Michigan is home to ten native turtle species. Not sea turtles, like the giant ones in Oman, but smaller turtles that lived in the woods and in lakes.

Smaller Turtles

1. The state reptile is called a "Painted turtle." On the front of

the brochure is a picture of
a painted turtle sitting on a log,
staring into the sun.

2. Snapping turtles have long
tails and white skin under their
chins.

3. On May 23, World Turtle Day,
Michigan celebrates with Turtle
Festivals and Turtle Story-telling.

4. Box turtles have polka dots on
their undershells.

5. Wood turtles are enormous,
not small at all.

Aref stuffed this one brochure into a suitcase pouch.

The other things he wished he could take—
his whole room, his friends—would not fit

into a suitcase of any size. He couldn't take his bicycle. Which made him think: I would rather be riding my bicycle than packing. For sure, for sure!

He could hear water running. His mom was in the bathroom taking a shower. Aref rapped on the bathroom door lightly and shouted, "Mom, I am going outside for a minute!"

"Come back inside soon!" she yelled. "And stay on our street."

His bicycle was tucked behind the dark red blooming bougainvillea bushes on the side of the house. An English name was painted on its back bumper, FAST FORWARD.

He clicked his red helmet under his chin, and coasted down the road next to his house.

His parents always said they were lucky not to have too much traffic on this street, which was why they had given him permission at the age of seven to ride on his own block up and down whenever he wanted. How much traffic would there be in Michigan?

Construction workers on a noisy yellow bulldozer were pushing sand and gravel off to the side of an empty lot. They waved to him and he quickly raised his right hand in greeting. They wore yellow hardhats similar to his helmet. One of the workers called out to him, "*Deer balek*—be careful, son!"

A dump truck paused over at the side. Dust spiraled up from a huge hole that an excavator was digging. He didn't know exactly what they were building. Probably just another house. But he wished: a candy store? That would be good. It could be standing there, a striped surprise, when he returned.

He swooped down a tiny section of pavement that went nowhere, as if once someone had planned to build a house there and quit. He stopped his bike at the end of the alley, staring out over the valley of houses, moving vehicles, tiny moving people, and bright sun cascading down upon everything—and beyond it all, the sea. He tried to imprint this scene on his mind, then began backing up, slowly, from the end of the alley, to the street, where he turned around again. "Why, why, why?" His mind clicked along with his pedals.

Sometimes moving backwards was important. Aref wished there could be one day, maybe Mondays, when everything moved backwards, as a sort of time experiment changing the view. You could eat dinner in the morning and breakfast at night. Cars could only reverse. Or you could eat dessert first at every meal. Wouldn't that feel like a different world?

Sometimes, even though he was old, Aref walked backwards swinging his arms, making a back-up beep, like a bulldozer or truck would make. You saw differently when you walked backwards. Aref had read a book backwards, put his shirt on backwards to see how it felt, and tried to write his name backwards. It looked very strange. English started at the left and moved right, Arabic words started at the right and moved left. What was backwards to one was forward to the other.

Would he feel backwards in Michigan or just the same as he felt in Oman?

He was pedaling hard. He knew where the

cracks were. He knew the best place to make a fast swooping circle and turn around. He knew where the bump rose in the street in front of Ziad's driveway and today he pedaled hard up over it so his bottom rose from the seat and the wheels jumped into the air.

Ummi Salwa was standing in her doorway moving her arm out and back to her chest, beckoning to him. She had a hard time speaking above a whisper now—she said it was because she was 100, but her voice was still deep and musical if you got close enough to hear her.

"*Marhaba*, Ummi Salwa! Hello!" Aref shouted. She smiled and waved harder.

Aref placed his bike down gently by her walk and ran up to her.

"Are you still here?" she asked.

This was very very strange. He could imagine what Sidi would say: "No, I have already left, I am gone now. You are having a dream."

"Yes, I am still here," Aref said politely. "My father left, but my mother and I are still here. We are packing. We are leaving in a week."

Ummi Salwa reached into the side pocket of her silken housecoat and pulled out a package of four tangerines and a small box of chocolates. "I wanted to give these to you, my son," she whispered. "May Allah bless you and may all the days be kind to you."

Aref surprised himself by taking her hand and kissing it. He had never done this before, but Sidi always touched her hand to his forehead. Kissing it just seemed like the right thing for Aref to do at that moment. "Thank you, Ummi Salwa," he said, also in a whisper. "I will think of you and look forward to seeing you when we get back."

She closed her eyes. Sidi had told him that Ummi Salwa could fall asleep while standing up now, but Aref didn't know if she was asleep or not. Maybe she was just counting up to the age she would be when he returned. Or praying. He walked back to his bicycle, placing her gifts in his basket. He should probably take the chocolate home, so it wouldn't melt. He looked back to wave, but she had stepped inside.

He made one more big zigzag down the street and coasted smoothly into his driveway. He was sweating now. He opened the door, and placed the gifts on the kitchen table.

Cat Without a Map

"Did you pack anything yet, *habibti*?"

Aref thought of the turtle brochure and his gifts from his friends and said, "Yes." He pressed his forehead against the cool refrigerator. "Will I feel backwards in Michigan?"

"What are you talking about?" His mother turned to him. "Sweet boy, of course not! You'll feel perfectly at home!"

"How do you know?" This was Aref's favorite question. He had now asked it one million forty-two times in his life, since he could talk.

"I just know." She put Ummi Salwa's chocolate in the refrigerator to harden it again and asked if he wanted a tangerine. He shook his head. "I think I'll have one, then," she said, peeling it with her fingernails.

She took a bite. "Ummmm—juicy. You know, Aref—even Sultan Qaboos went away from Oman to go to school. He went to England. It was long ago . . . and he came home. In our country it is quite a tradition that people go away, then they come back home. We can be proud of it."

Mish-Mish pressed against his leg. He would miss her so much. No one else seemed properly worried about this. Mish-Mish might forget him. "Do cats have good memories?" he asked his mother.

"I think so," she said. "I think that a cat can walk a very long distance to find its way home, so it must remember things. Remember a few months ago when I told you about a cat that got lost in America when its family took it on a trip? Why you would take a cat on a trip, I still don't know. The poor cat jumped out of the car at a rest stop and disappeared. It started walking on its own and unbelievably traveled safely across two hundred miles of Florida to find its old neighborhood. Can you imagine? All that way, and it ended up a mile or two from its house. It was gone two whole months! But don't worry, Mish-Mish will like Hani and Shadi too."

This made Aref feel worse. What if Mish-Mish tried to walk to Michigan? She'd get lost in the desert. Also, he didn't want to share his cat. Hani and Shadi, whom he used to enjoy playing with, were starting to seem like big trouble. "I hate them," Aref said. He ran to his room. His head still felt hot.

Aref's mom followed him and said, "My darling, you need to change that thought. You know it is not true. We do not hate anybody. They are your cousins and you love them very much."

Aref shook his head. "I used to," he said. "Now I only like them a tiny bit. Mish-Mish is my cat!"

His mom was staring at him with her serious face.

"Okay, I am sorry." He shook his head.

"That's better," she said. "You know Mish already likes more than one person in this house. She won't hate us just because she likes them. She can have more than three friends!"

He could smell the sun left over from his bike ride in his own swirling hair.

And there it was, his suitcase, still open wide on the floor.

His mom left the room and returned with some neat stacks of folded laundry. She placed them on his bed. "See," she said. "Easy! Just start putting these in!"

Aref wanted to kick something. He moaned in an odd way, like a faucet with a problem.

His mom sat down on the bed. "Aref, it's not a good time to be grouchy, you know. It's a good time to accomplish our chores and feel excited."

Maybe if he didn't pack, he wouldn't really have to leave. He slumped around his room, in front of his mother. Sunlight poured through his large window. A giant palm frond from the tree outside waved up and down. The shadow was like an arm directing traffic on his rug.

"You could pretend we are in a movie," Aref's mom said.

That seemed a little interesting. "What do you mean?"

"Haven't we seen movies in which people pack and get on airplanes and fly off above the sea and kiss the ground when they get to their special destination and everything is fun? Remember that movie about the flying bears? Didn't they do a little dance when they got off the plane? Aren't you excited about the airplane?"

"Not really." Aref remembered that movie. It was for babies.

"But you've never been in an airplane."

He was thrilled about the airplane, actually.

"Dad said there are movies in the backs of the seats and you can pick which one you want to watch. The remote control and the volume are in the handle of the seat—doesn't that sound fun? There's a whole list of movies, some especially for kids."

"Can I watch whatever I want to?"

"Yes! If it's for kids. And he said our apartment is perfect. It has a balcony that looks toward the swimming pool and a nice purple couch and striped chairs and our bedrooms have drawers built into the walls and it even has pans and a teapot in the kitchen. We weren't expecting that. He is making a list of things we will need to buy—like new rugs for inside the door and more towels and a big pot for soup. It will be fun to go shopping when we get there."

Shopping was rarely fun. Aref suspected only grown-ups found it fun.

His mother patted his head. But Aref wasn't a baby anymore and he didn't like it. "I still don't want Hani and Shadi in my bedroom," he moaned softly. "I'm sorry, but it's true."

She laughed. "They will take care of it. Trust me. And maybe you will have two windows in your new room instead of just one, wouldn't that be nice? You could do your reading for school out on the balcony, because there are chairs and a table out there, and it won't be so hot, like here. And when the snow falls in winter, you will see something very unusual. The snow will be fresh and soft—you'll be able to go outside and build in it. A snow person with a face and a hat! Maybe we'll get to see those giant snowplows clearing the streets. In the summers, you'll be able to walk right out our apartment door and dive into the swimming pool. You always wanted a swimming pool, right?"

"But we won't have the beach."

"No. We won't have the beach. Not our beach, anyway. The Great Lakes have their own beaches. Lake beaches. I think the sand is different shades of color in different places. Maybe they don't have waves, but in summer you can swim there too. It's a little drive from Ann Arbor."

Aref shook his shaggy brown hair. "I don't

think they will have waves. And I still don't think I will like it there, no no no, I don't."

He liked "no" in English even better than he liked "la" in Arabic—they meant the same thing. But "la, la, la" sounded like a song and "no" felt stronger now. He was glad to be speaking English because he didn't feel like singing.

Get Me Out of Here

Aref placed the folded laundry straight into his suitcase without looking at it. He figured, if he had been wearing these clothes lately, he must like them enough. They must be the right size. He opened a drawer and pulled out his brown swimming trunks with yellow and green turtles printed on them. Boom! Into the suitcase!

He didn't own a coat, but his mom said

they'd get one in Michigan. Oman never got very cold. His dad had told him that Michigan was sometimes called "the Mitten State" because of the way it was shaped, but Aref didn't own any gloves or mittens either. He didn't have a warm hat or a scarf or boots.

He packed his blue school sweatshirt with TAISM's—The American International School of Muscat—eagle mascot on it. Then he took it out again. He might need it before they left. Yes, it was true. He already knew a lot of Americans because he had been going to the American International School from the beginning. So, why was he so worried? They were all nice to know. Till now, he had been welcoming them to *his* country. And he had never had two extra thoughts about it.

You met new people, you made new friends. What had changed?

He had been practicing drawing eagles in his notebook. He sat down and drew two more with a sharpened pencil, wings outstretched. One had fierce eyes and the other looked a little silly, like a comedy eagle. See, this was the problem with packing. You got distracted by the things you were trying to pack.

For lunch he ate a peanut butter and honey and banana sandwich, and drank a tall, cool lemonade, then took a nap the size of Montana. He hadn't really taken naps since he was about three, and he didn't plan on falling asleep now—it just happened.

His mother woke him up about an hour later. "What are you doing? Are you getting sick?"

"I just got bored." Mish-Mish was curled on the bed beside him, tucked in the circle of his arm. She was purring loudly, as if she were snoring.

"Well, wash your face and wake up, Sidi is on his way."

So Aref washed his face and grabbed his rain stick and went to stand in the driveway and wait for Sidi.

The temperature on the thermometer said one hundred and twelve degrees. This kind of heat made Aref feel strong. Heat was silent and huge. No one could control it. People might cool their rooms, but they couldn't banish heat outside. The mint leaves curled up in such intense heat—the metal on a car or bicycle would shimmer. Heat made Aref feel like a cookie baking—something inside his brain puffing up proudly and slowly.

He banged the rain stick against his leg. In music class they had made instruments using regular household items. It was a fun day. He made the rain stick from a paper towel roll with dried white beans inside. He had tightly taped both ends of the tube with yellow duct tape and drawn blue birds with wide wings on the outside.

And the power it had! Rattle, rattle, rattle against his leg and around the bend, magically appearing, the clackety green jeep that his Sidi called "Monsieur." Aref could hear the jeep even before he saw it, since the engine was very loud with a distinctive grumbling sound. Sidi pulled into the driveway and stepped down from the high-up seat wearing his long white *dishdasha* and chunky brown sandals that he had made himself when he still ran his sandals shop. He was tall and he had a trimmed white beard and thick white hair combed back.

Sidi opened his arms and announced in Arabic, "*Ma-lish!* As you wish! At your command!" He hugged Aref a little harder than usual, the white fabric of his robe surrounding Aref like wings. "How is my boy?"

Aref usually spoke Arabic with Sidi. "*Ana mish mabsoot!* I'm not happy! Everything seems a little nasty right now, but—I am very happy to see you. So, I am a little happy."

"How's your suitcase doing?" Sidi said. He looked around the front yard and raised his arms like an eagle. He loved stretching and bending.

"It's doing bad. I can't fit any good things

into it. Just stupid things, like underpants."

"Trust me, underpants are important," said Sidi, looking serious. "What doesn't fit?"

"My friends, my school," said Aref, even though at that moment he mostly wanted to say, "YOU." "My blanket, the Mutrah Souq, the sea turtle beach, the caves."

Sidi listened closely. He put his hand on Aref's head.

"What I really need to take," Aref continued, "I wouldn't be able to close it."

"I'm going inside to say hi to your mom," said Sidi. "Then let's get out of here. *Yallah.*"

Peace to All Sardines

From the top of the hill where they turned off Aref's street, they could view the sea gleaming, intensely turquoise-blue in the distance. The closer they got, the bigger it grew.

Aref and his grandfather drove down to the beach without speaking much. Traffic was heavy around the LuLu Hypermarket grocery parking lot. "The whole city of

Muscat must be hungry today," said Sidi.

They parked near some concrete benches and beds of orange flowers. Instantly, things felt better. From here the beach stretched to the right, speckled with white umbrellas and fancy hotels. To the left the sand was wide open and more empty. Some kids were pitching a red ball back and forth with their dad while their mom jiggled a baby. Sidi handed Aref a chilled bottle of water. Aref popped open the lid and took a huge drink. Sidi thought of everything.

Aref placed the water in the cup holder for a moment and slipped off his tennis shoes. He stuck his socks inside them. "May I leave these in the jeep?"

Sidi said, "Please do." Aref decided to leave his rain stick in the jeep too.

They started walking and passed the family with the ball. Sidi said something to the dad, like *"Ahlein!"* or "Beautiful weather" or "Blessings on your family." He always talked to everyone. The sand felt compact, easy to walk on. It felt cool on Aref's feet. Gulls were dipping and diving over the waves. Farther out, some bigger birds, maybe flesh-footed shearwaters, held their mighty wings aloft and coasted. Aref dashed ahead and jogged around Sidi, then came back to walk calmly beside him again.

"I'm sorry about your hard day," said Sidi.

Aref didn't answer.

"We all have them. It will go away."

Aref still didn't say anything. He was taking giant steps and gazing off to the water.

"Did you know that our coastline is as long as California?" asked Sidi.

"Where is California?"

"Come on, even I know that one!"

Breezes rolled onto the beach. They lifted Sidi's *dishdasha*, which swirled around his ankles.

"Hello!" Sidi talked to the air too. "Breezes of India, thanks for cooling us off over here!"

"I wish we were going to India instead," Aref said. "Don't you? It's closer." He waved both hands to the side, toward India, like he was dancing.

The sky loomed with a few delicate lines of wavery cloud, one under the other. It looked like another blue ocean over the watery blue sea. Aref took a deep breath and tried to hold all the blue inside his body, pretending for a moment he didn't have to move away or say good-bye to anything or share his room and cat, none of it. He leaped into the air as high as he could, then did it twice again and ran in another wide circle. A cluster of sandpipers scuttled away from him.

Fishermen waved at Sidi and Aref from small wooden boats. Some were paddling and others were pulling nets of shining sardines behind them. "Are those men your friends?" asked Aref, catching up with Sidi again. Sometimes he went with Sidi to the fish market farther down the beach and Sidi ended up talking *forever* with the men in the stalls. Aref wasn't sure if these were the same fishermen or not.

Sidi said what he always said: "Of course! Everyone is my friend!"

Now Sidi called out to each boat, "Salaam! Peace!" They probably couldn't even hear him from that far away. Aref laughed. He knew what Sidi would say next.

"Peace to all people!" It was what he always said.

Then Sidi turned to Aref. "Aren't you glad you aren't a sardine? The sardines have a scary time when those fishermen with their fancy nets get out there! Peace to all sardines!"

Tourists walking in the other direction with picnic baskets and umbrellas stared at them now because Sidi was speaking very loudly like an announcer and waving his arm. Some men with red skins and blue swimming shorts passed them and tenderly lifted up their fried hands to say hello.

Aref twirled in a circle, making a bird sound. It was not hard to impersonate a seagull, but gulls always knew the difference. He would try to sneak up to them but they would open their wings and fly away without even turning around.

"If everyone is your friend, can we visit Sultan Qaboos before I leave?" he asked.

"He would have to invite us."

Last year, when the Royal Oman Symphony Orchestra musicians were playing outdoors at Amerat Park, Sidi had pointed out Sultan Qaboos in the distance, in a high viewing balcony above the other seats, wearing a beautiful, shiny golden cloak and turban. This was the closest Aref had ever come to him. Sulima had seen him from a distance at the grand opening of the Royal Opera House too.

"Promise me you will not go see him with my cousins when I am gone," said Aref.

"Don't worry. They're too bossy. I won't take them," said Sidi, laughing.

Looking

Puffy cottonball clouds floated over the beach. An airplane tipped one wing high in the distance, headed to Yemen or maybe Nairobi. Sidi walked slowly because his legs were antique. He looked around at everything with great, hungry interest, which made him walk even slower. He looked up and down and out. "There are turtles way out there that we can't see," said Aref.

"I'm sure there are," said Sidi.

Then Sidi said, "I heard something very interesting. You know what happened long ago? When the sultan's grandfather's father was living, long before electricity? People attached thick candles to the backs of large turtles. I guess they stuck them on with melting wax, then they released the turtles to roam around in their gardens and patios. So at night the wandering turtles became roving lamps carrying little lights around. Wouldn't that be something?"

"Were the turtles scared when they did this?" said Aref. "Could we try it?"

"I don't think it would be allowed anymore. We are protecting turtles these days, remember?"

"But would it hurt them?"

"It seems a little risky."

"I wish I could see it."

"Close your eyes."

Aref closed his eyes and pictured reading a book from the light cast by a giant flickering candle stuck on the back of a turtle. The patio would be filled with slow-moving shadows.

"It would be weird," he said. "And dim."

"But amazing."

"Yes."

Aref and Sidi passed a deflated pink floaty ring with a dragon's head. Sidi stared down at it. He picked it up and said he would throw it away. He veered off toward a big trash receptacle. Aref ran out into the shallow waves to cool off his feet. Far on the horizon, a sleek cruising ship with many windows lining its sides drifted silently. Who was in there? Where were they going?

Sidi looked back to see what they had already passed. Sidi had taught Aref to do this too, when he was little. Look at something ahead of you in the distance, then look at it when you get right up next to it, then turn around and look at it again when it is behind you. Sidi said it was important to get all the different views.

Possible Birds You Might See

1. You might see Little Ringed Plovers dipping.

2. Little Green Bee-eaters swooping.

3. Pipits pipitting.

4. Skylarks soaring.

5. Red-rumped Swallows flashing.

6. Flamingoes, geese, ducks,

swans waddling around together
looking for sardines.
7. Indian rollers with their
turquoise wings and heads
making everyone say, "Oh!"
8. Black-bellied storm petrels
circling.
9. Storks, spoonbills, herons, egrets,
pelicans, grebes, ostriches, saying,
"Hi Everybody."

It was really amazing how many different birds you might see.

You might also see trash, which was all made by humans, not birds. Not one bird left trash.

Possible trash left by humans
1. Water bottles, juice cans

2. Torn tickets, an oar broken
in half
3. The flat dragon
4. A purple plastic bracelet
5. A red striped baby tennis
shoe

Sometimes Aref went on beach trash pick-ups with his class and they always collected bags of strange mixtures of objects. Once Aref had found a really ancient coin with the picture all crusted. Sulima found a small hammer with a loose head and they tried to smash the barnacles off the coin to see if it was valuable.

Aref held Sidi's hand the way he used to do when he was a very little boy. The sky softened from bright blue to dusky darker blue. It looked as if a rainstorm might be coming. "We didn't need my rain stick after all," Aref said. "Good thing I left it in the jeep."

"I don't think it's going to rain though," said Sidi. "I listened to the radio. The radio weather report isn't always right, but you know how excited they get when there is going to be rain. I didn't hear them say anything."

Two geese flew over, squawking loudly. Birds always knew if it was going to rain, or anything else. A man in bright red jogging shorts passed them huffing and puffing, his skin slicked up with sweat. Aref lifted a stick of driftwood with a sharp point and wrote *Sidi* in Arabic on the sand. He wrote *Aref* in English. Then he made a bright sun with a face next to both words. Two gulls flew down and seemed to be staring at his work.

Aref turned to see the long, crooked beach tracks stretching out behind them. Both gulls were still nosing around. Aref took a deep breath. "I just don't know why I can't stay here, Sidi."

"I know. It's sad. Change is hard." Sidi had a very serious look on his face. "But think of it this way—if you stayed here, your parents would miss you too much. They would not be able to function."

One of the gulls ran up and stared at them as if it were listening.

"I think that isn't true," Aref said softly. "All my parents like to do is study."

Big Day

"Maybe you can find me some special treasures in Michigan. Look for more old coins like that one you gave me, and bottle caps. Don't forget that I love mysterious things that wash up on beaches. Even lake beaches. I don't know anything about those. Maybe you'll find a message in a bottle." Sidi had changed the subject. This was one of his specialties and Aref liked the way he did it, though it sometimes made him grumpy to have one of his complaints left dangling in the air.

Once, Sidi and Aref had written notes in Arabic and English, stuck them into a small green bottle, taped the top shut with heavy tape, and flung it out to sea, but they never got a message back from anywhere.

Today Sidi said, "Remember our bottle? I think the fish are keeping it in their library."

He bent over and picked up a flat gray stone. He pulled out the black permanent marker he always carried in his pocket, along with the tiny strand of wooden prayer beads his father had given him, and his keys. He held up the stone and drew a shy smile on its flat surface. He gave it two eyes looking off to one side.

Aref pressed the warm stone to his cheek.

He slipped it into the pocket of his blue jeans. "*Shookrun*, Sidi. Thanks," he said.

Sidi then picked up a brown stone with gray speckles curved on the top and a plain section on the bottom, like a half-and-half ice-cream cone, and drew a round mouth on the plain part saying *O*. "This stone is surprised," he said. "It thought it was the prettiest stone, but no one even looked at it for three hundred years. One day in 1838 the Sultan's great grandfather stepped right over it. Today is its big day."

Aref laughed. "My bad day, its big day."

"Pack them in your suitcase! You can think of the waves that carried them and listen to the stones whispering—come back to Muscat!"

Aref juggled them together in his hand.

They felt warm and made a nice click.

"Do they really say that?"

He lifted his hand to his ear and pretended to listen.

"Pssss, psssss, psssss. I think they are speaking Russian. Oh no, it's stone language. Yes, yes they do say that. Come back."

Aref slipped them into his pocket happily. Now his pants felt big and bunchy on that side but he liked it.

What makes a place your own? What makes a home a home? It wasn't something simple, like a familiar bench, or a fisherman's yellow sweater vest with a hole in it, or the nut-man's fat red turban. It was more mysterious, like a village with tiny stacked houses, so many windows, and doors with soft flickers shining out into the night. You weren't sure who lived in any of them, but you felt you could knock on any door and the people inside might know some of the same things you knew or welcome you in—just because you all belonged there. They might tip their heads and say, "Oh yes, aren't you that boy with the stones in his pockets? You want some soup?" and it would be lentil soup, which you loved. Or maybe it was how the beach air smelled—salty and sweet in whirls. You didn't have to do anything to feel comfortable here. You just walked outside, took a long breath and thought—*Yes. Sure. Here I am.*

Faces

The only hard thing about going to the beach was leaving it. "Do we have to?" asked Aref, running circles around Sidi as they walked the long ladder of steps back to the jeep.

"My knees say yes," said Sidi. "They need a rest."

On the way home, they stopped at the Sim-Sim Nuts Store, down by some other little shops that sold toys and sink faucets and car parts. This was their favorite place to stop when they felt a little tired.

"Let's get roasted almonds!" said Aref, hopping down from Monsieur.

Sidi was unable to hop at this point. He put one hand on Aref's shoulder and stepped out very slowly.

Najib the Nut-Man weighed the almonds on a balance scale, then poured them into a brown paper cone. They ate them all the way home. Sidi said they tasted smokier than usual, but Aref thought they were perfect. When they got home they offered the rest of the cone to Aref's mother, and she poured them into her little glass bowl shaped like an open shell in the middle of the coffee table.

Sidi stayed for dinner. They ate braised

cabbage and roasted potatoes and fish from the almost bare freezer. That night, after Sidi went home, promising to return the next day, Aref's mother came into his room to check on his packing, and say good night.

"Aref, I see stones in your suitcase," she said. "I thought you were packing up your rock collection to leave here. You can't take stones to America!"

"I have to," he said.

"They're too heavy! Imagine how many stones you will find when you get there?"

"They're my friends. Sidi gave them to me. Look at their faces."

His mother shook her head and poked around in the suitcase. "I thought you wanted to take a flashlight and a few favorite books and your playing cards and . . . what

is this? You're taking your rain stick?" she
said.

"Thanks for reminding me," said Aref.
"I'll gather those other things tomorrow."

Harmony

After his mom had turned out the light and pulled up the sheet and kissed him goodnight, and Mish-Mish had stood on her hind legs to stare into his face, then hopped onto the comforter beside him, Aref got out of bed again. He pulled the curtains back and gazed through the window at the distant water tower and some sailboats with loops of lights strung from their masts and thought about his grandfather. Sidi's memory was very deep. He really remembered the days before electricity came to Oman, when everything was lit by kerosene lamps or tiny bulbs run by generators or candles in cups. Matches were precious then.

Sidi remembered when all the roads of Oman were dirt or gravel or sand. He remembered when there weren't any tourists or people from other countries living in Muscat. You couldn't buy cheese from France or apples from Italy at the grocery store. Now there were students in Aref's own class from Denmark, Thailand, Iraq, the United States, Palestine, India, and Scotland. His school choir was called "International Harmony."

It struck Aref that he had never wondered too much about how his friends from

Denmark and Mexico felt when they moved to Oman. Did they feel the way he felt now? A little nervous and worried? Had he ever asked them how they felt or if they were homesick? He wished he could go back in time and do this. He wished to go even further back and see how dark the world was before electricity.

Now there were giant floodlights at the schoolyard and tiny lights along sidewalks and that blinking light on top of the water tower. But there were no turtles in any gardens with candles stuck to their backs helping people see where to step.

How Quickly
a Mood Changes

 The next day Aref woke up feeling strange again. He sat at the kitchen table swinging one leg, fiddling with the edge of his place mat, rolling and unrolling it. Usually he loved hot *zaater* bread with olive oil for dipping and fresh apricots, but not today.

"What's wrong?" asked his mother. She was polishing a tray, which seemed a strange thing to do first thing in the morning. "My happy boy is not so happy."

"I am in a very difficult position," said Aref slowly. "No one seems to appreciate this. I am not a happiness machine, by the way."

His mom had her orange scarf knotted tightly on her head. He knew that meant she was in an active mood—this was the work-scarf she always wore when she planned to get a lot done. It was like a warning sign at the beach—BIG WAVES! STAND BACK!—and usually meant bad news for him.

"*Habibti*, could you please sweep the kitchen and vacuum the living room carpet after you eat?" she said.

"At your service, madam." Aref had heard this on TV. "I will eat one apricot fast as light-ning, then I will do the chores with the speed of a desperate mongoose."

She raised her eyebrows at him. "Was it hard for you to sleep?" she asked. "My brain felt so full, I lay awake till three a.m. Then I got on the internet and read the local news in Ann Arbor, Michigan. About summer camps for children and a big local parade with bands playing and a new bookshop—but maybe it was a bad idea—my brain started ticking faster."

"Lovely," he said. He sighed, in the old man way.

"Wouldn't you prefer feeling excited too? Our great journey looms nearer every minute. . . ."

He wished he could feel like a pirate. Maybe he needed to wrap a scarf around his own head and get his ear pierced.

"Why does everything in our house have to

be so clean if we're just leaving?" he asked.

"People keep stopping by to say farewell. And you know I want things perfect for your aunt and uncle and Hani and Shadi when they move in."

Aref broke his apricot into two parts and plucked the seed out. "Madam, this apricot is mushy!" He placed it back on the plate and covered it gently with his napkin, as if it were dead. He plucked a banana from the fruit bowl and peeled it slowly and deliberately, as if it were the last, most important banana in the world. Would the bananas in the United States taste as good as the bananas in Oman? He didn't know anything.

When birds migrated, they carried all they needed to know inside their feathered wings, and small bodies. They inherited some astonishing compass inside their brains—same with butterflies. Birds knew how far to fly in a single day and where to land and where it might be safe to make a nest. Turtles knew this too. Turtles knew the exact moment to crawl out of the sea and make a nest on the beach.

Aref did not have this gift. Aref did not feel *this is the perfect moment for me to leave home and crawl up exactly 7,283 miles away on the shores of Michigan.*

His mother was unexpectedly dialing the phone. He could hear her saying, "Good morning! How are you? How is everything? How is the universe? Aref is going to do his chores in a moment, which might take him a while, but he woke up without an appetite, feeling gloomy again and I was wondering . . . what about an overnight? Didn't you mention that last week? Would it work out for you? Could you really take him camping? Eat lunch on the way? You don't mind? I need to get so much done in the next few days and he's not being the best assistant."

Yes!

Aref danced with the broom, then the vacuum; he wrapped a few more malachites and crystal stones, rearranging them in his rock collection box; he pitched some rolled socks into his suitcase; he crumpled all his math homework papers into balls and threw them into the trashcan, making a game out of it. He scored one hundred and fifty points, more than he had ever scored in math. He took a shower and washed his hair with mint shampoo, and got dressed for a camping trip in his old soft jeans and navy T-shirt with stars on it. He stuffed another T-shirt and some fresh underpants into his blue backpack.

Then he stood outside in the driveway waiting for Sidi and Monsieur to pull up. He looked down the street at the quiet houses and palm trees and blossoming yards and parked cars. A gardener was rolling a wheelbarrow filled with dirt into the driveway of the newest house down the block. The bulldozer men weren't even working yet. Their big yellow bulldozer and digger stood in the empty lot, patiently waiting.

A clean-up day had suddenly turned exciting. It was amazing how quickly a mood could change.

Delicious Detours

Aref's mother came outside to wave them off. She had a mop over her shoulder and a wide smile. "Have fun! Be safe!"

Sidi backed out of the driveway, looking into his mirror closely. He announced, "We are going to the Night of a Thousand Stars camp! You wore the perfect shirt. Remember when we went there a few years ago, but had to leave quickly because of the sandstorm?

Remember the baby camel that kept licking your head?" He turned right at the corner.

Aref laughed. "The baby camel thought I was its mother. No, father. That was crazy. Sand was getting in its eyes so it couldn't see clearly. It is probably grown up by now."

"It is probably in Saudi Arabia, drinking tea," Sidi said, stopping at a traffic light. "Do you have your toothbrush?"

"Yes! I even have underpants!"

Sidi laughed and said, "It is always fun to have an expedition, no?" Now he turned left toward the brown hills and mountains and the white ribbon of highway heading out of the city. A giant oil tanker truck lumbered past them going in the other direction, making a huge roaring sound. They passed gas stations, and a falafel restaurant, and a store for furniture and lamps. They passed a high school with a soccer field and a water filtering plant.

"Can we pass by the turtle beach?" Aref asked.

"On our way home," said Sidi, "we'll see what's happening with the turtles. We'll find out if any remember us. Right now we're going to drive up the road through the wild olive trees. Keep your eyes open for vultures. I'd like to take a turn to see one old friend on the way, if it's fine with you."

"Is his name Mohammed?"

Sidi laughed. "In fact, it is."

All Sidi's old friends were named Mohammed. Mohammed was a very precious name. In fact, Sidi's own name was Mohammed—but Aref never called him that.

"How long will we stay there, Sidi?"

"Not too long. Just long enough to get gas and chewing gum and sesame crackers and guava juice and sit on a big rock and ask Mohammed how his life is going. Later we will find a secret cave filled with prehistoric bones. . . ."

"Really? Bones?"

"Not really. But last time I drove up here, I saw a cave that might have some. Would you like to check?"

"Can we look for fossils too?"

This was the way they talked for miles and miles, syllables unrolling with the pavement. Were those goats or sheep? Well, maybe both, goats and sheep probably got along fine in the field. Did they speak the same language? Aref liked the large goats with horns. Near a tiny house beside an old stone well, blue towels flapped on a line. A girl wearing a red dress ran through a golden field carrying something yellow, like a stuffed bear.

Sidi and Aref rumbled along in Monsieur till the city felt far behind them.

"Look at that house," said Aref, pointing at another run-down little house the size of one room. "Who do you think lives there?"

"Obviously someone older than me," said Sidi.

To the left, up among some huge brown boulders, a truck seemed abandoned. "Why is that truck sitting in the middle of the field?" asked Aref.

"A hopeful uncle got lost searching for precious gems."

"Where is he now?"

"At the bank."

A white school bus passed them going the other way. Three large white vans followed the bus. "Looks like a field trip," Sidi said. There wasn't too much traffic headed toward the mountains, though.

"What's that smoke over there?" asked Aref. Large plumes floated over a distant slope.

"It's not smoke. It's dust. I heard they're building a new fancy neighborhood way out from the city, with good views, and the houses will all have swimming pools."

"We will have a swimming pool in Michigan," said Aref. "Did I tell you that? The other night, I thought I heard a wolf howling. Or maybe it was that fox in our neighborhood—Ummi Salwa told my mom she saw it sitting in the moonlight on her porch."

Sidi said, "Hmmm, did she open the door? I heard there have been more wolves spotted in the northern wilderness lately . . . but if it's in the city, I think it is a fox. Do foxes lick themselves the way cats do? I don't know that, do you? Do you think of a fox as being more like a cat or a dog?"

"A cat. But a wild cat."

"I think it's in between. I think it's just itself, not like either of them."

The jeep was hardly a smooth ride, but Aref loved it. He pretended he was riding a horse. Sulima took horseback riding lessons at the Muscat Equestrian School and Aref had gone with her parents once, to observe a special display of proud Arabian horses (wearing flower necklaces and headdresses)

doing tricks and jumps. Sulima loved it, but Aref's parents had never wanted him to ride a horse. They were afraid he'd hurt himself.

Aref gripped the door handle and fiddled with the radio with his other hand. Voices floated in from outer space. He liked the crackling, the scraps of messages and music that didn't really connect. Arabic and English and Farsi mixed together when you flipped quickly from one station to another.

They heard a faraway voice mentioning "A NEW MUSEUM!!!" and Aref said, "Where do you think this is coming from?"

"Abu Dhabi—for sure," Sidi said.

Aref twiddled the dial, letting more voices crackle out.

"Basra! Bahrain! Doha!" said Sidi.

Monsieur rumbled past long lines of palm

trees and wadis. They passed an ancient sand-colored fort with holes in the walls. In the distance loomed an old blue-tiled mosque with a minaret. They sang a bird song in Arabic, with a chorus of "Cheep! Cheep! Cheep!" and Aref clapped his hands. Sidi snapped the fingers of one hand. They waved at people driving in the other direction and those people waved back.

And sure enough, just as Aref had known they would, they took detours. They turned down a tiny road near a donkey stall and stopped at a field so Sidi could collect some stones that were orange, speckled and strange.

"I think these fell from another planet," he said. "They were meteorites that hit the earth. They came blasting down when I was a boy and split into pieces. I have always meant to stop. And look! So many. Still here."

Sidi dropped one into Aref's hand and the other stones into a canvas bag in the back of his jeep. Aref stared at his chunk of meteorite, which seemed very fresh despite being so old, and whispered, "Hello, outer space. Hello, faraway galaxies."

When they pulled in at Mohammed's shop, which seemed to Aref to sit too far off the road to have any customers ever, there was bad news for Sidi—another man named Sami was sitting behind the dusty counter. He said Mohammed caught a ride into Muscat to check on his foot.

"*Harram*, what's wrong with his foot?" Sidi asked.

"If he knew, he would fix it!" said Sami, and the two men laughed together.

"Well, tell him my two feet stopped to wish his foot well," said Sidi, "and Aref's feet did too, and we will come back another time, in three years maybe."

"I will tell him," said Sami. "I am sure his foot will be grateful. Would you like some falafel? I just made a fresh batch."

Sidi bought two steaming hot falafel sandwiches, which they ate outside by a chipped green plant pot shaped like a frog.

Then they zoomed down the golden-brown highway like two meteorites speeding through the heavens. It was incredible how much energy a falafel sandwich could give you. Sidi put on his sunglasses and sang a song in Arabic about a beautiful day and sunshine bathing the ground. Aref noticed the jeep rising to a higher altitude, its nose tipping up, up.

Before they got well into the mountains, Sidi pulled over to check out a watermelon stand. Ripe chunks of deep red watermelon were displayed on a table with a plastic cover over them, like a transparent tent, keeping off flies. The watermelon man seemed to be sleeping in his plastic chair. He jumped up and offered them samples, which were sweet and ripe and juicy. Sidi bought a watermelon and placed it on Monsieur's little backseat.

"Seen anything interesting lately?" Sidi asked.

The watermelon man told him some giant white cranes had been gathering behind the village at a pond, at sundown. The babies had already hatched, but the nests were still there.

"You think there might be any around the pond right now?" Sidi asked.

The man shrugged. "Don't know. You could go and look." He pointed behind him to a small road Aref hadn't even noticed. Aref and Sidi took a little hike that way.

Down the road lay a village of a few scattered houses, brown as putty or mud, and behind those houses was a shining pond as round as a coin. Some people stepped out of their houses to wave at them.

At the pond, Sidi spotted a few large nests of woven reeds and sticks tucked by the banks. Sidi motioned Aref to come over and said, "Look! Maybe they'll use them again for their next eggs." But not a crane was in sight. Sidi glanced around the bright sky. "Bet they're off having lunch like we did. Or maybe they've gone to another country too. Did you know that sometimes the father cranes sit on the nests just like the moms? They share the job. Have you ever heard a crane making wild trumpet sounds at dusk?"

"No."

"Well, we'll put that on our agenda. To come back here someday and hide in those tall reeds over there and wait for them. Good idea?"

"Very good."

Almost Lost

To get to the Night of a Thousand Stars camp, they had to drive through more brown mountains, green valleys and curvy passes, then off the paved road into a huge desert. There were still mountains all around. Sidi paused for a moment, looking out carefully, to make sure this was the place to turn. Then he drove straight onto the uneven golden sand. It felt strange driving without a road.

"This looks like the moon," Sidi said, as he steered with mighty effort, turning the wheel hand over hand. Monsieur careened forward.

"How do you know that?" asked Aref.

"It's how I dream of the moon," said Sidi. "No signs. No roads. Just a huge blankness."

Aref stared at him. "I look at the moon, but never think about *being there* on its surface. Do you really dream of that?"

"Of course," said Sidi. "I am secretly an astronaut. Except—oh right, I don't like to travel. Never mind."

The jeep seemed to be slipping and sliding in the sand.

Sidi turned the wheel hard to the left. He held it tightly.

"Are we okay?" Aref asked.

"I remember this strange part of the trip

from the other time we came here," Sidi said. "It goes on for a few miles."

"It seems really long," said Aref. He was gripping his door handle, jostling side to side.

Monsieur stirred up a big sandy dust cloud—some of the dust came in through the windows, which made Sidi cough. He stopped driving till he finished coughing. "We'd better close these windows all the way. Sorry, I know it feels as hot as a stove with them closed."

Sidi looked to the right and the left. Then he stared at his compass with the big black and white face attached to the dashboard.

Aref couldn't see any camp anywhere. "Are we okay?" he repeated. "Where are we? What direction do we want?"

"Southwest. We might be lost."

The sand stretched out like a giant

sea—rumpled and brown and deep and entirely empty of trees or other vehicles or people. A ring of mountains still surrounded them. "It's huge," Aref whispered.

"And it's not dead, either," said Sidi. "Some people act as if a desert is dead, but it's very alive and constantly shifting and changing."

A string of camels, some big ones and some smaller, like teen camels, gracefully crossed along the top of a dune way up ahead of them on the horizon. They walked in a perfect line, as if they had very good manners. But Aref knew camels sometimes got irritated if people made them carry things and walk for a long time. All of a sudden, they might go berserk and start spitting. The camel that had licked his head out here three years ago was very sweet, though.

Aref wished they could talk to the man who was riding on the first camel, and ask him for directions, but the caravan was too far away. Another man who looked like a shepherd in a flapping cloak walked behind the line of camels.

"I wonder if they take turns riding," said Sidi. "Maybe not. I wish I could talk to them, find out where they're going or coming from . . . I wonder if they're Bedouins. See that fat saddle-bag under the first one? They're carrying their pans and food and water in there. Their blankets. It's their suitcase, all wrapped up. Everything they need, so they can camp at night. He's sitting on his traveling suitcase."

"Should we hike over and talk to them?" asked Aref.

But Sidi said it was getting too late. He

didn't want to be lost in the desert. The sky turned orange and puffed. The camels shrank into little moving spots.

Finally, when Aref was really starting to feel a little worried, the Night of a Thousand Stars camp appeared in the distance, with its loops of glittering white lights strung from posts and a few thin, deserty trees scattered around as if outlining an oasis. "There it is!" Aref cried, very happy the long drive was almost over.

Sidi parked Monsieur beneath a crooked desert tree. He took a deep breath and said, "Yes! I was getting worried. Did you know that? Could you tell? I tried to hide it. I thought we might have to sleep in the jeep. And that is not good sleep. Jeep sleep."

No Roof

It was strange to arrive anywhere new. You felt awkward for about ten minutes, then felt yourself sinking into the new scene, becoming part of it very quickly.

Aref sat down on a green wooden stool that turned out to have one leg shorter than the others, so it rocked. He switched to a small blue chair and adjusted it on the hard earth patio decked with small metal tables. Sidi chose a larger red chair with yellow flowers painted across its back rung. The chairs had flat cloth pillows on them. Some people from England were eating and drinking at another table. Three older Omani men in *dishdashas* and hats sat smoking a hubble-bubble in the corner, speaking softly in Arabic. One was rocking in a rocking chair. Sidi raised his hand and nodded to both groups.

An Indian man named Naveed greeted them. "Welcome! How was your trip?" He complimented Aref's starry shirt. "In a few minutes you will see even more stars in the sky—keep looking up!"

Sidi held out the watermelon to him. "My friend, we brought you a present."

Naveed bowed and looked happy. "My favorite!" he said.

Naveed was wearing a yellow turban. He brought them lemonade in clay cups on a tray. "I will be back momentarily with the rest of your food." Then he served them curried vegetables and mounds of very fragrant rice and hot bread on large clay plates. Aref was extremely hungry. A fire blazed in a pit lined with stones. The desert became chilly the moment the sun went down. Aref stared at the sinking sun with a softly hypnotized feeling.

"Oh my!" said Sidi. "This is delicious! My stomach is happy! And my legs are cheering in relief, to be out of the jeep!"

Aref wondered, where had this food come from? Was there a cave in the earth filled with secret refrigerators? Did a helicopter fly low overhead and drop food supplies down in a basket attached to a parachute? It was very mysterious. When Naveed returned to ask if they would like second helpings, Aref hadn't even finished his giant pile of rice yet.

Sidi put his hand over his stomach and said, "I am grateful, kind sir, but no. How long have you been out here, cooking all these tasty dinners for wanderers?"

Naveed laughed and shook his head. "Time runs together. One month, one year . . . I think I have been here almost two years. Or maybe since the beginning of time! My brother used to work here and I took his job when he returned to India for his marriage."

"Were you scared when you came?" Aref asked.

Naveed smiled kindly. "No. The desert is a friendly place."

Far in the distance, at that exact moment, they heard a weird scream. It didn't sound friendly at all.

"What's that?" Aref asked.

"The hyena, " said Naveed. "Big teeth." He opened his mouth hyena-style to show them his own teeth.

Aref shuddered and asked, "Does it come close to this camp?"

"We hope not," said Naveed. "No, I think not. I think you will not be seeing it, no." He was shaking his head to make Aref feel better.

"Don't worry, Aref," said Sidi. He was smiling and didn't look nervous at all. "Their voices are much scarier from a distance than close up. If you meet one, they act scared of you."

"Is it like a wolf or a fox?"

"A little bit, yes," said Naveed.

Sidi sat comfortably in his red chair moving his prayer beads quietly through his fingertips. He looked peaceful. "We came here once before," he said, "when this boy was younger . . . your brother must have been here then, but we didn't get to spend the night because a sandstorm was whirling up."

"No sandstorms tonight," said Naveed. "Very quiet!"

Right then, the hyena howled again and everyone laughed.

Sidi and Aref washed up in the camp bathroom, a little square building made of brown cement painted with a single dark blue frill around the top of the wall. It had no roof on it. They could look right up at the twinkling stars with no trouble. Amazingly, a single silver faucet offered a stream of cool running water.

They brushed their teeth standing side by side. Then they stepped out of the bathroom and stared up at the sky some more. The Milky Way stretched and glittered like a massive white sparkling ribbon. It cast a softened glow across a great canopy of sky.

"Oh . . . I see some beautiful planets that I haven't seen since before we had lights," said Sidi. "We slept on the roof all summer long when I was a boy and the Milky Way poured its stories down on our heads and into our dreams. . . ."

"I want to do that, Sidi," Aref said. "You always talk about it. Can't we still do it?"

Sidi pointed out a distant planet with a reddish-orange tint and said, "I think that's the one we used to wish on. Yes, we could still do it. We could put two cots or mats up on your roof or mine. You could spend the night at my house before you go. Why not? Why haven't we been doing that? We forgot! Air conditioning makes people forget."

They walked slowly back toward the patio. One of the English men was playing a guitar near the fire pit and singing softly. Sidi and Aref stood for a minute and listened. Aref had heard this song before, at school. "Turn, turn, turn." Aref mouthed the words.

Naveed guided them to a black-and-brown striped camel hair tent on a raised wooden platform. They would sleep on cozy narrow beds covered with dark purple and blue stitched quilts. An old red rug covered the floor, and some large maroon satin pillows sat stacked in the corner. Aref raced around investigating. He pointed at the bed farthest from the door. "That's my bed!" he said, thinking of the hyena. "This one's yours." He patted Sidi's quilt.

Sidi sat down on his bed, smiling.

Aref opened a drawer in the small wooden table between the beds and pulled out a flashlight, clicking it on and off. A kerosene lantern on the table flickered softly. Their huge shadows danced on the tent walls.

"I like a bed inside a tent," said Aref. "It seems better than a bed in a house. Why don't we live in tents all the time?"

"Good idea," Sidi said. "When you come back from the United States, we'll both turn into Bedouins."

"We'll change our names."

"We'll change everything."

"We'll cook soup in a big pot over a fire."

"We'll learn how to play the guitar."

"When I get old enough to drive the jeep, we'll travel back here and ride camels instead. You can sit on the suitcase."

They climbed into their beds. Aref blew out the lamp.

Sidi snored.

Sidi the Sphinx

In the morning, very loud desert birds were chattering wildly in the skinny tree branches right outside the tent. Birds did not talk that loudly in Muscat.

Aref wanted to take a shower in the bathroom without a roof. The water was so cold, he screamed like a hyena. His shower was extremely short. He ran back to the tent wrapped in a towel to get dressed.

"Why were those birds so noisy?" he asked Sidi as he shivered inside the towel.

"They were cheering for morning."

"Why?"

"They like it."

Aref pulled on his sweatshirt from school—thank goodness he had brought it. They stepped out of the tent onto the small platform, then the sand. The desert air was surprisingly cold. "Give me your hand!" Sidi said. "My legs are so stiff! I am becoming a Pyramid. No, more like a Sphinx. Or let me lean on your shoulder—here—ow—I think I got a leg cramp from standing up crookedly this morning."

It was harder to walk on drifty sand than on pavement, if you weren't used to it. Desert sand wasn't packed hard, like sand at the beach.

"What are we going to do now?" Aref asked. He felt like running or doing a cartwheel.

Sidi raised both his arms high in the air. "Here, please join me in exercise," he said. "I am doing my morning stretches. They are keeping me flexible and young."

Aref copied him. Sidi began moving his arms in high circles like a windmill and Aref did the same. They tipped their heads from side to side, stretching their necks. "Ahh, doesn't that feel better?" Sidi asked.

They walked back over to the green metal tables and chairs in the camp's dining area and Naveed greeted them. "Uncle! Good morning! Would you prefer coffee or tea?"

Aref thought it was funny how he called Sidi "uncle."

"Can I run for a minute?" he asked.

"You can run for ten!" So Aref took off, making a big looping circle out into the pliant sand and looking back on the camp. He saw Sidi pointing to another line of camels crossing the top of a distant brown sand dune. Aref counted them—seven. The camels looked straight ahead when they walked. This group had only one shepherd, not two. Where were they going? They weren't headed to Muscat, that was for sure. They were headed in the other direction. To Yemen, maybe.

They sat back down at the same round metal table and ate the scrambled eggs, which tasted delicious even to Aref, and flat bread and watermelon chunks that Naveed served them.

"You are a magician, brother!" Sidi said to Naveed.

"I like eggs now," said Aref.

They pitched little breadcrumbs to a hopping bird with black-and-white polka-dotted wings. Naveed was making coffee for Sidi in an old-fashioned fancy metal pot over the fire. The English people had disappeared.

"They went looking for birds very early," Naveed said. "I sent them to the stone ridge at the second dune." He pointed beyond the high point where camels walked.

"Bird-watching?" asked Sidi. "Well, we are bird-watching right from our chairs. Or maybe the birds are watching us." A smaller, speckled-wing bird landed right on Aref's foot, peered up at him, and flew away again.

"Look at him," said Aref. "He's so curious. He doesn't seem frightened at all."

"Why would he be frightened?" Sidi asked. "We never hurt him. We only feed him."

"So he likes us," said Aref. "I like him too. He could be my pet. But he wouldn't enjoy Mish-Mish. Let's stay here forever, Sidi. Let's live at this camp."

Sidi put his hand over Aref's. "I love it too. But this camp isn't going anywhere. It will be here when you return. First, you have to go on your journey. Your parents are so proud to attend a famous graduate school and you will enjoy your new school . . . it will be fun. Everyone in your family will be going to school at once."

"I would rather stay here!"

"Don't worry, you will come back. In three years, you will be back."

Aref was blinking hard to keep the tears inside his eyes. How many were in there, anyway? Were eyes little factories that made as many tears as you needed?

"I want to be with you," said Aref. "Every single day."

Sidi shook his head as if he were going to say "no" but instead he said, "Of course! You will still be with me. Always. Study hard and tell me what you learn. Find me some rare American rocks. Make your father mail them to me. We'll send messages all kinds of ways."

There was a long silence in which a desert wind as huge as a highway blew right past them. Sidi closed his eyes. "Listen to that," he said. Aref put his head down on his folded arms on the table.

"You can tell me about American policemen and basketball and muffins," said Sidi. "I heard they have a lot of muffins over there." Aref didn't say anything. So Sidi went on.

"Or maybe, you could tell me about the lakes and . . . maybe you will meet some fishermen. I wonder if they use nets or not. I will practice my e-mail techniques and turn into an expert for you."

This made Aref laugh. "No, Sidi, I don't believe you!"

Sidi shook his head. "Trust me, it will not be easy, but I will do it. I will even go to a computer class at the library if I have to. Then every single one of us will be going to school."

Aref turned his face away, wiped his eyes, and felt a tiny bit better. Sidi gave him hope, anyway. They could still stay connected.

"Why don't you take another little run before it gets too hot?" Sidi suggested. "I'll just sit here and watch you. I'll do Aref-watching instead of bird-watching. Run in a big circle around the camp—see what it looks like from the camels' point of view."

So Aref took off again, jogging. He headed up toward the dune. Since the soft sand absorbed each foot deeply, he felt as if he were running in slow motion, sinking a little with each footfall. A circle of birds flapped up from the brushy spot where they were nibbling, leaving little puffs of dust. A speckled brown lizard family stood in a circle with their heads together, having a morning conversation.

Aref looked back at Sidi sitting in the chair, watching him. He waved. Sidi, his white beard gleaming, his shining damp hair combed back, raised one hand and held it in the air. Aref blinked. Right then he knew that moment was clearly written in his brain forever.

No Missing Feathers

When Aref returned from his triple circular jog, huffing and puffing because of all that sinking, Sidi handed him a triangular white stone with crooked lines engraved across its surface. "See this? It's the map of the run you just took. See, there's where you turned and came back. I found it under my chair while you were running."

Aref took the stone and held it between his

palms. "It's so hot." He stared at it. The criss-crossing lines really did look like a map.

"Now look at this!" Sidi said, pointing off to the right.

A man they hadn't seen before, wearing a leather jacket and red pants with fringes, was walking toward them with a giant falcon sitting on his shoulder. The falcon had a leather hood on its head and was sitting upright and still, with wings tightly tucked at its sides. Aref had seen falcons before, but he'd never met one personally.

"*Marhaba*—hello!" said the man. "My name is Jamal. You like to meet my friend?"

"*Walla*—sure!" said Aref.

Sidi greeted Jamal, who said, "I am staying at the camp for a week, doing some training with my bird."

"Were you here last night?" Sidi asked.

Jamal shook his head. "We weren't sleeping—we were off on the ridge staying awake for many hours."

Aref knew this was how a trainer disciplined a falcon—they both had to stay awake for a long time till the falcon took orders properly. It seemed a little extreme.

Sidi looked interested. "Aref, did you know the falcon is the fastest flyer in the world?" he asked.

"Of course," said Aref. "They can peck your eyes out too. Their beaks are very strong."

"That's true," Jamal said. "My friend's name is Fil-Fil—pepper—for the spots on his wings." He took Fil-Fil's hood off. Aref stepped two paces back, without thinking.

When Jamal made a clucking sound with his tongue, Fil-Fil shot off his arm like a rocket. He soared in the direction the camels had gone, becoming a distant spot. He glided high, then dipped lower and shot up again, circling twice, and zooming back toward them—a wildly speeding blur. It appeared he could change directions like magic, swooping and veering. Coming closer again, Fil-Fil circled their heads.

Aref covered his face. "Yow, that's too CRAZY!!!!"

"Look! Look!" said Jamal. "Watch what he does now!"

Jamal whistled sharply. Somehow, Fil-Fil put on his bird-brakes high in the air, curled around, dipped down and managed to land perfectly on Jamal's arm. He tipped forward to catch his balance, then rocked back and was still. Sidi and Aref looked at each other and opened their eyes wide.

"You want him to land on your arm?" Jamal asked Aref. "You want to hold him?"

"Sure!" Aref said, after a second. He felt a little scared when he said it.

"He is the smartest bird I ever knew," said Jamal. "I have known many falcons personally, but Fil-Fil is outstanding. He flies farther, faster, and always comes back instantly to my command. We were just having an intense training session the other night because he was making up his own rules. Please notice, he seems proud to meet you. He likes it when people watch him fly."

Jamal pulled a second leather landing pad

out of a pocket in his jacket and wrapped it around Aref's arm, fastening it tightly with some strips of cloth. Aref blinked. He stared at Fil-Fil's huge, hooked claws.

Jamal placed his large arm alongside Aref's much smaller one and clucked to the falcon. The bird stepped over onto Aref's arm, staring straight into his face. Aref took a deep breath. He slowly turned his face to Sidi. "Look!"

"He's excited," said Jamal. "He wants to fly some more."

Sidi was watching everything closely, not saying a word.

Jamal made a tiny whistling sound and Fil-Fil expanded his speckled wings, opening them wide as if displaying their glory. Then Jamal clucked again. Fil-Fil rose up with a strong spring into the air. Aref's arm fell hard when he launched. Fil-Fil zigzagged, soared, dipped, curled, and circled.

"He has the gift of motion," Sidi whispered.

"In a minute, I'll tell you to lift your arm to invite him back," Jamal said to Aref. "But let him fly a little more first. He has so much energy."

"Did you hear about the Falcon Hospital in Abu Dhabi?" asked Sidi. "They have two hundred air-conditioned rooms for the birds."

"Yes," said Jamal. "And they also give the birds passports when they leave, declaring them healed or cured of whatever problem they had. I am glad to say Fil-Fil has never had to go there for any reason."

Now Aref wanted to go there, just to see

it. What would it feel like to be able to spring into the air and soar with your own body, no airplane beneath you, nothing? He knew that even the loss of a single feather could destabilize a falcon—sometimes, at the bird hospital, a falcon who was missing a feather or two had to have some other feathers stuck or sewn back into its wings, so it could regain flying balance again. They had talked about all this in his science class, studying birds and animals of the region. He wished his whole class were here right now.

Fil-Fil dove dramatically. He swooped around and zoomed into the sky for two more wide circles. Aref, staring up, realized he was panting.

"Raise your arm!" Jamal instructed. Aref gulped and lifted his arm. Fil-Fil swooped toward him and landed cleanly, as if they had been practicing for weeks.

"I love it!" Aref said.

"My heart is pounding," Sidi said.

Then with little murmurs, Jamal coaxed Fil-Fil onto his own arm, bowed to Sidi and Aref, and carried him to the side of the patio, to a falcon roost Aref hadn't even noticed the night before. He put the hood back on Fil-Fil's head, and attached his leg to a large ring on the roost, with a clip-on leash.

Naveed came out from his own small tent and started clearing the rest of the breakfast dishes away, as if nothing unusual had just happened.

"Thank you, Jamal!" Aref said. "That was really fun!"

"We do thank you, friend," Sidi added.

"Meeting you and your bird was a big surprise."

Jamal placed both his hands together in the Indian greeting way, though he was an Arab speaking Arabic, and bowed again. "I am going to take a nap," he said. "Since we were up all night, Fil-Fil and I."

"I'm stronger now," said Sidi, who hadn't said much at all for at least ten minutes. "That falcon gave me strength. Poor guy, staying up all night to learn his lessons. Let's walk out into the desert a little ways. I feel warmed up."

They headed toward the dunes, on a reddish path of gravel and sand. Sidi kept his hand on Aref's shoulder for balance. The growing heat of the desert seemed round and full.

More black-and-white birds darted down
from the tent rafters and sailed along beside
them. Aref wondered if they were scared of
falcons. Maybe they had been hiding. The
camels had completely disappeared. Aref
wished they would come back. Sidi kept
sniffing and urging Aref to smell the air and
breathe deeply. "That way, your body will
carry the desert back to the city," he said.
Aref gulped and held his breath.

When they turned around and starting
walking back to the Night of a Thousand
Stars camp, Aref stared at the whole picture
before them—small tents, purple pom-pom
doorways, brown stucco bathroom, painted
green stools, metal tables, and one tired
sleeping falcon. Everything glistened, an
oasis in the sun. He ran circles around Sidi,

saying, "I love this place! I think it might be my favorite place!"

"You will be like my falcon," said Sidi. "You will fly away and come back. Just as he did. That was beautiful."

One More Star

Falcons Take Naps Too
1. I was a little scared when Fil-Fil was going to land on my arm. But he was nice to me.
2. Maybe I could train my own falcon someday. I forgot to ask how people train falcons. Where do you get the information? Do you just watch other people?

3. I also forgot to ask if Fil-Fil ever pecked Jamal.

After pausing to watch some gigantic desert ants with huge eyes crawling into a round hole in the sand, Sidi and Aref spotted two new cars approaching, raising dust. Sidi opened his arms wide. "Welcome, lucky new guests. What a wonderful morning! We need to get our bags and make room in paradise for those people. I could stay for a week!"

"I could stay for three years!" yelled Aref.

Naveed had already rolled up their sheets and swept the floor of their tent. They gathered their things and headed out to say good-bye to him. Sidi reached into his deep *dishdasha* pocket, extracted a tight little roll of money and handed it over. "Here you go, with respect for your delicious food and hospitality! *Alif Shukran*."

Naveed bowed. "Thank you, *Alif Shukran Ammi*, please come back again."

They all bowed and nodded and smiled to one another. Fil-Fil on his perch seemed to be sound asleep under his hood. His perfect feathers weren't even quivering.

Between the cook tent and Monsieur, Sidi stopped and stared down at the sand at his feet. He bent his knees and stooped, groaning a little, stirring the sand with his fingers. "Did you hear my bones creak?" he asked, plucking up a black-and-brown speckled stone, which reminded Aref of the falcon's feathers and the little birds' feathers all at once. "Aha!" he said. "I felt it through the sole of my sandal!" He handed the stone to Aref. "Do you have one exactly like this? I'm not sure what they call it. Here is your reminder to fly away and come back again."

Aref stared at him and popped the stone into his pocket. "Thanks, Sidi," he said.

They walked to Monsieur with their bags and climbed in.

Sidi turned the key. The engine coughed and chugged. He paused and turned the key again. Aref patted the dashboard and said, "Come on, Monsieur, you can do it."

"There must be sand in the engine," Sidi said. But Monsieur finally woke up.

As they were passing under the arched NIGHT OF A THOUSAND STARS sign at the camp's gateway, Aref said, "So, Sidi, did you see a thousand stars last night?"

"Ah, now you remember to ask! No, I only

saw nine hundred and ninety-nine. So we will have to keep our eyes open for that last one. What about you?"

Aref just laughed.

Homeward, with Turtles

Driving out of the desert across the hills and gullies of sand was as difficult as driving in. Sometimes the wheels spun and the jeep made a whirring sound. Sidi wrestled with the steering wheel. "I thought I'd be in practice from yesterday," he said, "but today, the sand seems even shiftier. Doesn't it?"

Aref felt happy. Getting stuck was a real possibility.

"Did you hear the wind blowing last night?" asked Sidi. "Whooooooooooo—say, where DID our tracks go? Do you see any? I thought the road would be clearer in the light. And what about those people who just drove in—where are their tracks? I don't see any tracks at all! And what happened to those English bird-watchers? Maybe the camels picked them up and will give them a ride far, far away. Think of it—people traveling across deserts for centuries, finding their way by the sun and the moon and the stars. People staring up at the constellations for guidance—now that was smart."

"I wish we lived back then," said Aref. "Not now. I wish we still lived without cars and airplanes."

"Really? Then we couldn't move around as easily."

"Exactly."

Finally they found a paved road. Sidi wasn't positive it was the same one they'd been on yesterday. The sun was rising higher in the sky. Aref pulled his sweatshirt off. The sun was cooking him through the window.

"Sidi, do you ever get hypnotized staring at sand?" he asked. The brown tones of the hills and dunes were mixing and mingling in his eyes.

"Yes, I always get hypnotized. But I am still a good driver when hypnotized." Sidi laughed.

They were the only ones on the road. Aref liked the swishing of the jeep tires and the creak of the axle when the jeep hit a dip. Finally another vehicle went by. A white government truck, heading west, carrying—what? Hammers and nails? Fish food? Goat milk?

A school bus with a leaping gazelle on its side passed by. More summer school students on a field trip, maybe? Some of them waved at the jeep. Aref waved back, proud to be on a private excursion with his grandpa, but wondering what they were all talking about inside the bus.

Sidi pulled up in front of a crooked shop. Tangerines were piled in a pyramid shape on a display table out front. "Let's get tangerines!" he said.

Aref felt hungry too. "Do you think they have pumpkin seeds?" He wanted something salty.

Yes! The old man inside the shop poured a scoop of pumpkin seeds onto an ancient scale with balancing weights, then funneled them into a paper cone. Aref was licking his lips. The man added a few more and smiled at Aref. He did not have many teeth. He offered them fresh pomegranates from a wooden bowl. He asked Sidi if they could stay for lunch or have a cup of tea.

"Not today, uncle. We're on the long trip back to Muscat and this boy has to leave to America soon."

"Allah bless you," the old man said. "Come again!"

Sidi asked Aref to peel him three tangerines while he drove. "They stink," said Aref. "But I will." He wiped his hands on a dishtowel Sidi kept folded in the compartment between their seats. Aref really did not like the smell of tangerines.

A little farther down the road, an extremely old lady was sitting in front of a house. Next to her was a large wooden wagon piled high with yellow melons. Aref could see a melon field full of leafy vines stretching behind the house. How did she water it? Did she have a long hose? This didn't look like a place with running water. But wait a minute—there had been running water at the camp and it was more remote than this. Did she carry a bucket? She didn't look strong enough to carry a bucket. Maybe she had a deep well, like the camp must have.

Sidi parked near the wagon. "Let's ask if she has running water, Sidi," said Aref. "She looks even older than Ummi Salwa." He hopped out.

Sidi climbed out of the driver's seat very

slowly. He groaned. "Oh my, I thought I had stretched, but I am really too stiff. I am turning into a tree trunk." He pressed on one side of his back and bent to the left, to ease his muscles.

"Buy ten melons!" the ancient lady called out. "If you buy ten, you can have them very cheap!" She giggled as if what she had said was very funny.

"I am sure of that!" Sidi said, laughing too. "But no one needs ten, *hajja*! Only two—one for my grandson and one for me. We will pay the price!"

"Ten is better!"

"Two are enough! Say, where do you get your water for watering your fields?" He had begun selecting his two melons.

"I have a well that is older than the prophet's beard," she said.

Sidi poured some coins into her skinny hand. Aref noticed three cats peering out the door of her small hut, as if they hoped a fresh food delivery had arrived.

The lady stood up with great difficulty and hobbled over to the jeep. Aref worried that she was going to try to get in.

Sidi placed the two melons carefully on the backseat. He arranged their backpacks on either side. "We don't want them to roll around," he said. She peered into the jeep with interest.

"Can you stay for lunch? Would you like some tea?" the lady asked.

"Thank you," Sidi said, "but my boy here has to get to America and I am going to drive him. This jeep grows fins and swims when it needs to."

"I would like to see that!" she said. Now she coughed into her hand and squealed like a cat with its tail caught in a cabinet door.

Aref stared at Sidi.

"Allah bless you on your journey!" the lady said. She seemed full of energy.

"And you forever, kind grower of melons and teller of tales."

When they were back on the road, Aref said, "You talked silly to her."

"She needed it."

"Does anyone buy ten melons?"

"Only if they have ten children. Or can't count."

"Or are having a party. Or want to serve melons to the whole class."

Leaning with the curves of the road, they ate all the salty pumpkin seeds, cupping them in their hands. Sidi was careful not to go too fast. "I am driving more slowly because of snacking," he said.

Aref felt his feelings about juicy tangerines might be changing—when he peeled two more for Sidi, he felt inspired to eat one himself. It was a perfect combination snack. His cheeks and hands felt sticky and salty at once.

The day grew bright and hot. Sidi asked Aref to get his sunglasses out of his pack. "Now I am James Bond," he said when he put them on.

They passed three hikers wearing orange baseball hats, carrying orange backpacks. Everyone waved. "See how people love our country? They come here just to hike around," said Sidi. "It is exciting to them. You will feel like that in America."

They passed a broken-down wooden boat with no paint on it, abandoned next to the road. "How did it get here, do you think? Not even beside the water?" asked Aref.

"I think it had a hole, and someone dumped it."

"Maybe it is a famous boat from history waiting to be discovered."

"Noah's Ark?"

"Was that a real boat or just a story?"

"Or maybe this sad boat belongs to that wild donkey tribe and the donkeys have gone off to find a boat craftsman to repair its holes."

Sidi had just seen some donkeys in the distance. Now they were part of his tale. "Look! Look at that swirl of dust in front of the striped cliff! It's an oryx running! We are very lucky today!"

Aref leaned forward to see the oryx leaping out of sight. "Maybe the oryx and donkeys are living together over in a cave."

"They have started a secret society."

"Sidi, do you think geckos have a private language?"

"I do. I think everything has a private language."

"Even a tree?"

"Especially a tree." They were passing some bending palm trees at that moment. "And those big ants we saw in the sand? For sure they were communicating."

Talking with Sidi felt like a sky of floating words. You could say anything. Words blended together like paint on paper when you brushed a streak of watercolor orange onto a page, blew on it and thin rivers of color spread out, touching other colors to make a new one. Blue and red to purple, yellow and blue to green, drip and slide and shiver and BING, a new color. Just the way the sea looked, off in the distance now, shimmering like a full paintbox of deepest greens and blues.

Suddenly Sidi turned right off the road onto a flat spot of land and stopped the jeep. He clicked off the engine. There, spread wide before their eyes, a vast white beach. A few giant turtles sunning in the sand. Their backs were as big as small tables.

Sidi hadn't forgotten. "Ras al Hadd," Aref whispered. "The nesting grounds." Although he hadn't mentioned the turtles even once today, Sidi had taken a special detour to check on them.

A turtle was crawling out of the water

just then. "Is that a Loggerhead? A Green? A Hawksbill?" Aref knew their names, but couldn't always tell them apart.

"I don't think it's an Olive Ridley. It's too big," said Sidi.

If it were midnight during nesting season, there might be hundreds out there. If the babies were hatching, there would be countless tiny turtles scrambling around covered with sand. Aref knew that the Green Turtle would return to the exact same beach for egg-laying for *decades*. Turtles had invisible maps inside their shells.

"I think there's a better viewing spot up that little hilltop," Sidi said. "Come on."

Aref kept staring at the sleeping turtles on the beach as they climbed. Turtles weren't just cold-blooded reptiles. They were miracles.

Candle on Your Back

Were the sleeping turtles dreaming? Were they aware, through tiny reverberations in the earth, when cars, trucks and buses passed by on the roads? Aref had learned that turtles had intricate systems of tactile perception—they could feel the thudding of your feet on the ground, if you got close enough.

"I wish I could be here when all the

baby turtles crack out of the eggs," Aref said. "That is what I wish most." But it was summer right now and the eggs had already hatched. The babies were out there swimming around in the sea, going to Somalia, stopping for holidays on little islands.

Older kids from his school had talked about seeing the eggs hatch. They carried bedrolls and tents and spent the night in a camping ground at Ras Al Junayz.

Sidi had seen the baby turtles hatching long ago. "I know," he said. "It's one of the wonders of the world. I can't believe how smart those little turtles are, the moment they are born. They know exactly where the water is, by smelling it. They must have imprints inside their cells—turtle directions. No one has to tell them. It pulls them right in. And it pulls all of them back and back to the same beach for years."

"They are really smart."

"And think of all the things they have to avoid—crabs, birds, hungry foxes, people . . ."

"Their lives aren't easy," said Aref.

Turtle Life Is Not Always Easy
1. People hunt turtles for their meat. Yucko.
2. People hunt for turtle eggs in sand—this is all illegal !!
3. People hunt turtles for their shells to make stupid things that could be easily made from plastic, like eyeglasses and combs.
4. People hunt turtles for their

oil. ?? I don't really understand
this one but I read about it.
5. People hunt turtles even for
their leathery skin but my mom
said she would never carry a
purse or a wallet made from
turtle skin. Illegal, people!
6. The first turtles lived more
than 185 million years ago.
They saw dinosaurs become
extinct. Maybe this is why
they look a little like dinosaurs—
they remember them.
7. Fossils of ancient turtles
have been discovered in Oman.
8. Some people say turtles
allowed the whole earth to be
born on their backs. They were

here first. Anyone who does
something mean to turtles is
very, very bad.

Sidi was raising his head high like a turtle in the sun, pushing its neck far out from its shell. "Can you smell the water?" he asked.

"Yes. Can you?"

"Yes. We will come see the babies hatch someday," Sidi said. "I promise you. You may camp with your school, but we will also come together and stay longer."

"We will do everything," said Aref. He spun around on his tiptoes. The sand on the turtle beach was covered with wide turtle tracks.

Sidi pointed. "Look there, far up at the crest of the waves! When a wave rolls over, you can see big turtles inside it, paddling hard."

Aref looked and saw blurred, beautiful turtles, suspended in the moving water. It was a wet, blue-green world out there. The turtles were surfing inside the waves.

"Look! Did you see those red flashes over by the rocks? I think those were clownfish. I'm still thinking about that weird candle thing you told me," Aref said. "The candles on the backs of turtles. How did anyone ever think of doing that?"

"Well, it would be easier to do than sticking a candle on a falcon," Sidi said. "I guess they were just desperate for night-lights."

Now Sidi bent over and stretched his arms out again. He tipped to the left and to the right. "Ahhh, this feels so good for circulation. I am stiff."

Aref stretched his arms out too. The wind was blowing through their hair and clothes. "But I am not stiff, I am stuffed! We ate breakfast and then we ate all those other things!"

"Probably we eat too much. I am as stuffed as a turtle inside a too-tight shell."

"I am stuffed as a bed full of monkeys!" said Aref.

"I am stuffed as a squash packed with rice," said Sidi.

Aref laughed, picturing the cap of the squash, the tip-top with the stem end, pressed on Sidi's head like a hat.

"Okay," Sidi said. "That's enough stuffedness. Let's go back to Muscat. Home is calling." He leaned over and picked up one tiny, smooth, round white pebble and handed it to

Aref. "Here you go. A miniature turtle egg. From the land of the turtles."

Aref held the stone tightly. "We could stay in this exact spot until I am in sixth grade," he said. "We could pretend I went away and came back again. That would be good. I wish there were a button I could push. Just to stop everything right here. I don't want to leave the turtles. And then we'd see the babies hatching too. We would see every single thing the turtles do, except when they are underwater."

"That's nice. I like it," said Sidi, smiling. "It makes me remember something. Once when I was fourteen or fifteen, I wished for a Stop Button very hard. I was sitting in a pool of sun on the stone step at our old house, just a regular day waiting for my father to walk up the road after working, and everything around me and inside me felt—all the right size. I wished I could stay that age with my own thoughts and my father coming home soon. But it wasn't something you could say, really. You just carried it inside you. So, I know."

Aref looked out at the waves, then at his grandfather silently. He knew too. They walked down the hill and climbed into the jeep and drove away from the turtles. The turtles who carried their homes on their backs and swam out so far and returned safely to the beach they remembered.

To Drive After
Standing Still

Monsieur carried them past slopes and cliffs and hillsides. Craggy caves and purple flowering bushes. Mounds and curves and dips and sudden views of the sea and rough spots in the pavement and a broken wagon that looked like a cousin of the abandoned boat. They talked about this and that. When you drove out in the country, you felt closer to the earth than you felt in the city. You had better thoughts in the country. Your thoughts made falcon moves, dipping and rippling, swooping back into your brain to land. Maybe the motion of spinning wheels relaxed and enlivened them. Your thoughts weren't tied to one spot, and they weren't nervous, either. They were just open, and rolling. Maybe this was why some people decided to travel all of their lives, going to new places, not knowing what they would see next.

Aref slept a little, his head bobbing over to the side. Sidi played some Arabic music very softly on the radio.

The Candy Bowl
and Everything Else

As they entered Muscat, Sidi started whistling. He sang in a high pitch, "I see a stoplight, Stop, Stop, Stop light."

Aref shook himself awake. "Did I sleep? I didn't want to sleep!"

"Sorry to bother you," said Sidi, "but I knew you would want to see the historic landmark we are passing."

Aref sat up straight. There it was. Sidi's

funny old shop with the green and white awning and rows of brown sandals lined up on shelves behind the window. Aref knew how it smelled inside—smoky rich, like cut tanned leather. A man called Abu Pumpum was running the shop now, counting money, zipping it into a pouch. Pumpum was a nickname, not a real name. Sidi had sold the shop, complete with every single thing in it, to Abu Pumpum two years ago. Aref and his dad had gone with Sidi on the last day to say good-bye to the chairs and shelves and rulers for measuring feet and the candy bowl.

Sidi, driving very slowly, pulled to the curb. A large shuttle van beeped and roared around them. "Do you need new sandals from Abu Pumpum before you go?" he asked.

"No," said Aref. "But thanks. I wear mostly

tennis shoes now. I will have to wear snow boots over in Michigan anyway."

"People wear sandals there too."

"They do?"

"I am sure of it."

Cars were beeping all around them. Sidi pulled out slowly into the crowded lane, Monsieur chugging and the air full of city noise again.

"Do you miss running the shop?" Aref asked Sidi.

"I do. But now I have more time to play around with you and work in my garden and take naps."

They passed the stately white Marine Science and Fisheries Centre. "The last time I went there with my class," Aref said, "we saw turtle hatchlings scrambling around inside a big tank. The man said they were three days old. Soon they were going to be taken back to the ocean."

"So you have seen them already!"

"But not on the beach."

A woman stood at a crosswalk with a wide basket filled with bananas on her head. "I'm glad people still carry baskets that way," Sidi said. "I'm glad there are still donkeys in the *souk*."

They passed the sign pointing toward Sinkhole Park, which they had driven to more than once. "Remember when we climbed down those hundreds of stairs," said Sidi, "and I was clinging on to the handrail, while you ran like an oryx to the pool of water at the bottom? That was a steep climb! And I was even younger then. It was gorgeous."

"You want to go there again today?"

"Next time."

They paused at a long red light. Crowds of lunchtime workers in *dishdashas* and dresses, suits and casual clothes, crossed the street. Sidi pointed out a new block of yellow villas being built. "Look how they are putting blue tiles over the doors. I like that."

They were gliding past the giant library where Aref used to crawl on the floor under the tables while his parents studied. He learned how to read shoes first. Then he learned how to read books.

"Have you returned all your library books?" Sidi asked.

"Yes."

It felt cozy seeing what you recognized. Good-bye! Good-bye! Good-bye!

Ahhhhhhhhh

When they walked back into Aref's house, his mother said, "Now that's what I like to see, people smiling! How was the desert, you travelers? You wouldn't believe how much I've gotten done, both here and at the university. My colleagues gave me a little party and I became my own assistant and never stopped moving for a minute." She hugged Aref while Mish-Mish nuzzled his ankles.

"The desert was deep, as always," said Sidi. "And your whole house is smiling. It looks very fresh. We, on the other hand, are somewhat rumpled and smelly, but we had a great time."

Aref was jumping and teasing Mish. "It was wonderful!"

"Did you see camels?"Aref's mom asked. "Were you cold? Did Monsieur behave?"

Mish-Mish ran in circles around them, sniffing the desert on their clothes.

"Everything was perfect," said Sidi. "We saw camels, yes. Not close up as before. And turtles too and many small talkative birds, and something else which Aref will surely describe to you."

"The falcon! He flew so fast and came back to my arm. Mom, I got to hold him! And a black-and-white bird sat on my foot!"

Aref flopped down on the cool carpet and spread his arms and legs out. "Ahhhhhhhhh. Why can't I just keep going to school here? It would be so much easier. I could visit you in summers. I could live with Sidi. We could keep going on adventures."

His mother laughed. "Adventures! Get ready for the biggest adventure, dear heart. Your father says that people are being very friendly to him and he met some neighbors who also speak Arabic and they had a marvelous dinner together. There are children around your age who are looking forward to meeting you. Lucky boy!"

Aref was not very interested in this. "Why does everyone say I am so lucky?" he said. "I don't feel lucky. But our trip was *great*!"

Aref's mother handed Sidi a falafel sandwich with tomatoes and lettuce inside. Sidi ate it in four bites. She offered one to Aref, but Aref said, "No, thank you. Are you kidding? I am still stuffed!"

He placed his hands over his head.

"Do you have a headache too?" his mom asked.

"No, I'm just thinking. There is too much to think about. It's going too fast for me to finish one thought before another one comes."

"That sounds like naptime to me," said Sidi. "I'm going home now for a good rest. Thanks, traveling partner!" He hugged Aref a long time before he climbed back into Monsieur and clattered away.

Missing Something

Aref's mother had been busy. All the books and magazines had been cleared off the living room table. The photographs of Aref and his parents were gone. The half-burned candles had disappeared. The tables had been polished. The house was starting to look like a hotel.

Aref turned on the television. There was a program about large white cranes flying thousands of miles to their winter nesting grounds. They were smart. Were they even smarter than the falcons or the turtles? How did they do it? He looked closely. Were they flying to that pond he and Sidi had walked around?

That night before he went to bed, Aref made up a song. "No no no, I won't go. No no no, I won't go go go." He slapped his drum while he sang it. His drum was made of goat-skin and he had gotten it as a present from Sidi when he turned four. It had a leather strap he used to wear over his shoulder.

Aref tried sticking the drum into his suit-case, but it took up too much room. He lay on his back on the rug stretching his legs way out to the sides, as if they were turtle flippers.

"You are really funny," said his mother from the doorway.

"I am *not*."

"We have a good life here, I understand why you love it so much." She stooped down to kiss him on his forehead gently, turned, and pulled the door to his room, not closing it, leaving it just the way he liked, so he saw a thin crack of light coming through. He dove into his bed, pressing his face into the pillow that smelled like sun and air. His mother still dried sheets and pillowcases on the roof on a clothesline with pins, the old-fashioned way, and sometimes she asked him to go upstairs and bring them down when they were dry and he loved to hug and smell them filled with light.

Aref felt like he was missing something, but he wasn't sure what. Being a baby, maybe. He missed being a baby. He wished he were still lifted and held, words streaming around him. Babies didn't have to do much or explain anything. If they cried, everyone tried to make them happy. When you were big, you couldn't say you were missing this, though. It would make you seem as strange as a tropical fish with orange hair.

A Hundred Flavors

The next morning Aref's mom was bubbling water for mint tea when Sidi showed up. "Big news!" he announced. "I found one more tangerine in my pocket. Due to your new appetite for tangerines, I wanted to share it."

Aref laughed.

Sidi sat down on the couch, peeled the tangerine and passed a few juicy sections to him.

"I was thinking about something," Sidi said. "Would you like to spend the next two days at my house? Your mom still has things to do, and some final meetings at school, and I was thinking, maybe we could go on a boat ride. I could ask some friendly fisherman to take us?"

"Yes yes yes!"

"And then we will get a little tired of each other and you won't be so sad to leave."

"Not true!"

Aref grabbed his backpack again, which he hadn't unpacked yet, kissed his mom (who already seemed to know the plan) good-bye, and jumped into the jeep's seat. "Hi again, Monsieur!" He fastened his seatbelt.

Sidi lived down in the older section of Muscat, in one of the thick little houses that had existed before electricity. Aref always thought it would be fun to take a hike from his own house to Sidi's, but he hadn't done that yet. Sidi's white house had only three rooms, but they were very large and the ceilings extremely high, so your voice echoed a little inside. The entryway of the house had a nice swooping curve of tiles over the door, like a blue wave. It was an old-fashioned house.

Sitti, Aref's grandma who died when he was a baby, had sewn the ruffled yellow curtains that still fluttered in the open windows. Sidi liked fans better than air conditioning because he said they let the inside and outside worlds feel closer together. Sidi and Aref stepped out of their sandals and shoes at the door and entered. Sidi liked only bare feet on his clean floor. A big wind blew the curtains high like flags. "Look!" said Sidi. "It's Sitti welcoming you!"

"Hi, Sitti," said Aref.

Sidi started singing "The Happy Song," the song he always sang when Aref or his parents visited his house. His notes echoed off the high ceiling. The words had some curly parts in them, where Sidi would trill. Once when Aref was younger, he had asked his dad to sing "The Happy Song" before he went to sleep at home, but his dad said, "I can't. Sidi makes it up differently every time. No one else knows it."

On Sidi's dining table were two white plates piled high with fat purple grapes and cherries, Aref's favorites.

Aref started singing too. "I have a grape in one hand and a cherry in the other." Walking around the rooms, he let his voice lilt and quaver on the notes the way Sidi did when he sang in Arabic. He loved Sidi's soft blue blanket folded neatly on the bed, the antique kerosene lantern on the living-room side table, the little golden knob on the table's single drawer, the red wooden stool in the kitchen. "Why is your house always so happy?" Aref asked, knowing what Sidi would say.

"Because you're in it," said Sidi. "Don't you know that by now? What makes a house smile is—people. When they come in and out. When people talk and laugh together, the house is having a good dream."

Aref was quiet. He knew Sidi's philosophies so well. But hearing them again made him feel comfortable. So he asked, trying not to whine, "Will your house feel sad when we leave? Will our house feel even worse?"

Sidi shrugged. "The houses may cry—a little sorrow of peeling paint, a jagged crack in a corner—but they will wait for you to get back, the same way I will. Oh! I got you a present."

He handed Aref two postcards, one of the long white Ras al Hadd turtle beach and the other of camels striding across dunes, like the ones they had just seen from the Night of a Thousand Stars camp. "You can pin these to the wall of your new room, to help you remember everything," he said. "Make your new house happy."

"Why can't you come with us?"

"I don't fly. I am the falcon without wings and I must stay here to protect everything in the nest, remember? I have to guard the frankincense trees and the date palms. We have a special relationship. Anyway, Monsieur would cry."

Aref shook his head. His grandfather was stubborn and silly.

"There's one more present for you hiding in my bucket," said Sidi. "It's a better present."

"And where is the bucket?"

Sidi lowered himself into a chair, shrugging. "You have to find it."

Aref did one cartwheel on the deep red carpet. The thick rug felt good on his bare feet and hands.

He dashed into the bedroom and glanced around—bed, chair, small dresser with stones lined on a silver tray in the center—the bucket wasn't there.

It wasn't on the pale green tiled kitchen

counter or sitting in the wide white sink.

It wasn't hanging in the hall from the coat hooks.

"Where is it, Sidi?" he asked.

"Just keep looking!"

They had done this all of Aref's life. Sometimes Sidi hid new socks under a pillow. He hid a book about seaweed or Moray eels or a ticket to a movie. Sidi had even made treasure hunts with things as little as cherry tomatoes, now very popular, though Sidi said they hadn't existed at all when he was growing up.

And there, in the bathroom, under the shower spigot, right over the drain, in the center of the new turquoise tiles that Sidi was so proud of . . . was the silver bucket.

Inside it was a brand-new elegant blue hat

with stitched golden threads in an angular mountain pattern and a lush blue neck tassel. "For me?" Aref stared at them. He had never had his own dress-up tassel before.

The tassel was exactly like the one Sidi wore around his neck for special occasions. Sometimes he would even dip it into cologne. His dad had one too. Aref pulled his over his head.

Aref put the hat on and stared into the bathroom mirror. "It fits!"

He ran back to the living room. "Look! These are really nice, Sidi. Thank you!"

"Aref," said Sidi. "When you come back to Muscat, you will be a different boy. If the hat doesn't fit anymore, I will get you a bigger one then."

"I will not be a different boy," said Aref. "I

will only be a slightly taller boy."

"Right, you're right! I'm sorry! You'll be the same boy with some added new flavors. Didn't we talk about a boat ride? Let's have a snack, then go down to the docks and look for my friend Ziad or any fisherman with a friendly face."

Sidi went to the refrigerator and pulled out his big blue bowl of homemade yogurt. He made it fresh every few days. He spooned a glop into a bowl, drizzled honey on it, and sprinkled a handful of almonds over the top.

"I believe they have a hundred flavors of yogurt in the United States," he said.

"Like what?"

"Lemon with pistachios. Banana with peanut. Apricot with walnuts."

"Cinnamon with mustard."

"No!"

Aref took a bite of his delicious yogurt. "Sidi, what if I don't make any friends in the United States?"

"That would be impossible. Friends are everywhere. Aren't you friends with the people from other countries in your school?"

"For sure! But this is different. I will be the new one now. I won't know the same things they know. What if no one likes me? What if they make fun of my hat?"

Sidi patted his shoulder. "Then you can let them try it on."

Sidi Nets a Sea Stone

Aref and Sidi clattered over to the beach again in Monsieur. It was a shorter drive than from Aref's house. Some snorkelers were standing on the sidewalk near a beach hotel with fins and goggles in hand, looking out to sea. The sun was dancing on the water. Sidi drove past the hotels toward the fishing docks, pulled up and parked under a palm tree. "Let's hope for the best," he said.

They walked toward the water's edge and the bustle and clank of fishing boats. Nets were spread across the sand. A fisherman was stitching a torn net with a wide wooden needle and some string. Buckets and fish coolers were scattered around everywhere. The air smelled like fish.

Sidi waved at a fisherman. "There's Moussa," he said. "I buy fish from him sometimes. Let's give him a try. I don't see my old friend Ziad anywhere." Moussa, carrying nets and poles with one arm, waved back with the other hand.

"Hello, my uncle!" said Moussa. "I haven't seen you for a long time, where have you been?"

"Brother, I have been in the desert with a falcon and this boy here, my grandson, Aref.

We have a big question for you. Could we possibly ride in your boat with you for an hour? You're going out, yes? Would it be too much trouble for you to bring us back in?"

Sidi glanced at Aref. "I don't want to get stuck out there for ten hours or something."

"I do," said Aref.

Moussa looked as if he was debating this.

"I know most fishermen don't like to come back to shore so quickly," Sidi said. "But Aref is going to the United States very soon. I promised to take him out in a boat before he left. But I don't have a boat. I will make you a whole bowl of yogurt in trade for this favor. Or some *kousa mashi* or *makloubi* or whatever you like."

Moussa laughed. "You don't have to make me anything. It might be a little trouble to bring you back, but not too much. I've already been out and come in to shore once this morning. I'd love to have your company."

The sea wind blew a little harder. They were standing close together on the sand. Aref dug the toe of his shoe in. Moussa pointed at his boat tied to the dock, red with a sunburst of yellow painted at the stern. A single word was written in Arabic. *Mabsoot*—happy. They were going out on the *Happy* boat. Aref felt his hair flap up on his head like a wing.

Moussa walked over to the dock and out to the boat with them following. You could look down into the water here at the shallow edge and see some darting minnows or anchovies or sardines playing around together. Moussa loaded his equipment into the boat and adjusted some faded pillows on the crossbar seats. "We're all set!" he said. "Hop in!"

Sidi couldn't hop, but Aref hopped, then offered his hand to Sidi. Moussa helped Sidi too. The boat felt a little tippy until they all got balanced. Sidi and Aref were sitting side by side, Moussa across from them. Moussa pulled an orange life preserver from a box under the seat and handed it to Aref. It smelled musty and fishy.

"Sorry, this stinks. Do I really have to wear it?" Aref's eyes asked the question of Sidi, who answered out loud.

"Yes!" The jacket was a little big, but Aref pulled the straps tighter and snapped it on.

"Thank you for coming along, my uncle," said Moussa to Sidi. "It is my pleasure to host you both."

"And it is our pleasure to come," said Sidi.

A boat! Aref looked around him. He smiled at the fishermen in the next boat, who called out greetings when they saw him. A family strolled by on the beach, a red cooler dangling from the father's arm. A boy about Aref's age ran ahead of them. He stared out toward the water. Aref felt proud to be sitting in the boat.

Moussa undid the line tying his boat to the dock. He pulled the cord on the motor and the engine coughed and spluttered and roared into life. *Vroooom! Mabsoot* was moving. Aref held on to the side next to him with one hand and Sidi gripped the seat with both his hands.

"Son, have you ever been to India?" Moussa pointed out across the Gulf of Oman in the direction of India.

"I have not, can we go there today?" said Aref.

Moussa laughed. "It is much too far for today, but someday, yes, surely you must travel there, up and down, north and south, as the countryside is so much larger than our own people imagine. It is huge, and every part of it different. Well, I have not been everywhere, but India—a most amazing place! Streets are packed with people wearing bright colors, you hear ringing and clanging of bells as you scurry between curry shops, cows sleeping next to streetlights, tea stalls with elephants standing by—little bicycle taxis zoom wildly between everyone, as if stitching the traffic, on three wheels, passengers must grip on very tightly. Your eyes will pop out."

A larger green boat zoomed past them, causing waves, which made them grip on tightly too. "Sidi and I are going to go there someday," said Aref, even though he wasn't sure he wanted his eyes to pop out.

"Maybe in a bigger boat," said Sidi. "I like your boat, Moussa. It is rocking us like a baby's cradle."

"The ride will get smoother in a minute," Moussa said. But another boat passed them and the waves grew larger the minute he said that and crashed against the side of *Mabsoot*, splashing their faces. "Can you swim?" Moussa asked Sidi. "Shall I get you a life preserver too?"

"That is always a good idea," said Sidi. Moussa tugged another faded life jacket out from under the seat. Sidi stuck his arms in and clipped the belts in front. "Now we are all safe," Moussa said.

"What about you?" Aref asked. "You are not wearing a life jacket."

"I am a dolphin in disguise," said Moussa. "I swim like a dolphin and could ride a dolphin if I needed to. Have you seen any dolphins lately?"

"No," said Aref. "But we saw a LOT of turtles yesterday."

"Turtles! Kings of the sea! I could also ride a large turtle. They live even longer than we do sometimes. I bow to them! Have you ever gone deep-sea diving to see live coral beds under the water?"

"I think I have to be older to do that," said Aref. "But my dad and I went snorkeling once."

"Ah yes," said Moussa. "The great under-water mystery tour. When you get older, you can also ride a banana boat. Have you seen this one? It looks like—guess what? I haven't done it though. I prefer my boat to look like a real boat. Some people now have powerboat joyrides, wakeboarding, paddleboards, ringo rides, waterskiing . . ."

Now his real boat was rocking hard in the wake of a larger yellow boat motoring fast toward the marina. "Slow down, slow down!" said Sidi. He looked a little strange. The spray was drenching them.

"I would like to do everything!" said Aref, enjoying the shower, hanging on tightly. Salty drops dripped down his cheek and he licked them. Three sailboats were headed north, far out on the water. Aref liked the way they looked with their big white sails unfurled. Someday he was going to own a sailboat. He had decided that—right this minute.

"Then you are like our brother Sinbad the Sailor who had so many great voyages on the sea. Do you think he came from Sur or Sohar? Some people say he grew up in Iraq, but I think he was from Oman, don't you think so? *Walla, Ammi,* are you scared of the water?" Moussa asked Sidi, who had been very quiet, his head tipped to one side.

"How could I be scared?" Sidi asked. "I lived next to the sea all my life. Scared would not be the word. But my stomach feels a little . . . frisky."

Moussa reached into his pocket and pulled out a wrapped peppermint. "Try this, uncle, it will make you feel better. And please don't look down at the waves, look up at the sky."

Sidi unwrapped the mint and popped it

into his mouth. He tilted his head back and began staring at the sky very hard. "Thank you."

The sky, dotted with cloud puffs in long layering lines, stretching from Oman to India and countries beyond . . . the sky, a round dome, a big bowl, a feathery crown.

They had motored out beyond the hotels. Very tiny people were sitting on tiny bright towels around the swimming pools. They could see a fire pit burning at the Chedi Hotel, palm trees leaning and blowing and the white buildings of the city, pressed up against the dusky brown mountains. Everything looked peaceful and quiet, like a painting or a dream.

Moussa sang a few songs to them, old Arabic fishing songs, with curly notes and repeated refrains—songs about waiting and watching and being out in the water under the giant sky.

His face had a sunbaked toughness—Aref liked his face. Moussa threw his white net into the waves on the side of the boat by Sidi. It sank down into the water pulled by its metal weights. Sidi gripped the top edge of it where it hooked onto the boat. "I am in charge of the net," he said, in a frail-sounding voice.

"Would you like to hold a fishing pole?" Moussa asked Aref.

"*Walla*—for sure, yes!" Aref said, thinking, who wouldn't?

Moussa placed the pole squarely in his hands. "If you feel a tug, you do this," he demonstrated the knob on the spinny reel and showed him how to turn it very quickly, which Aref already knew. The reel made a clean whizzing sound, which he also liked.

"What do you want to catch?" Moussa asked. "Bluefish? Shad? I attached a lure that they both like. . . ."

Aref just grinned at him and shrugged. He knew some fish were bigger than he was. "I think any fish would be good," he said.

They all rocked back and forth together. The wind circled their heads, spreading out across the tops of all the waves. Aref wished one of his friends from school would pass by on another boat and they could slap hands from boat to boat.

Right then, Aref felt a tug. He stood, tried to turn the knob, jerked the pole backwards and lost his balance, slipping to his knees. He let go of the pole, but Moussa grabbed it in time. A shiny silver fish flapped into the air, then opened its mouth and dropped back down into the waves.

"*Mabruk!* Congratulations!" Sidi said.

"Lost it!" said Moussa. "He was quick! Here, try again!"

Aref stood up and shook himself off. He wasn't even sure he wanted to catch a fish because then the fish would be DEAD. Fish looked better flashing in the sunlight for a moment, then slipping back into the waves.

The sun got hotter and hotter. The motor was humming softly and the boat was circling and floating in place. "I think it's a good spot," Moussa said.

What did a fish think when it saw a fish hook with a pretty feathery lure on it?

Yummy, yummy, yummy?

Boom! Another tug. Aref pulled. He tried

to turn the reel with his right hand, but the tug against him was very strong.

Sidi grabbed Aref's waist so he could stay balanced. Aref cranked the reel slowly and then—the fish flew up above the water and— splashed down.

"Keep going," said Moussa. "Slowly, slowly . . ."

Aref turned the spool as steadily as he could. As the glistening silvery fish rose again, its head poking out of the water, Moussa added his strength to the reel and said, "Aref, you have a big guy here! This is something!"

The shining, spectacular fish flopped into the boat, its eye staring straight up at Aref, who wanted to pat it the same way he patted Mish-Mish. Its mouth was opening and clos- ing in a perfect *O*.

"Is it dead yet?" asked Aref.

Moussa said, "No."

"Can we let it go?"

"Why?"

"I want it to escape. I want it to have a longer life. Please!"

Moussa looked at Sidi and Sidi shrugged.

"I would make fish soup," said Sidi. "One or the other."

"We will do what you say, Aref," said Moussa, raising his eyebrows. "I'm sure the fish will thank you. Myself, I would keep it. But, it is your fish. You want to throw it back yourself?"

"Yes!" Aref was a little afraid to pick up the huge fish since touching it made it wriggle hard. And it was very heavy when he gripped it. "Tell the turtles hi from me!" he said as he held up the fish one moment, then dropped it cleanly into the water where it slid home, disappearing instantly.

Aref shivered, imagining its relief. "Sidi!" he called loudly, though Sidi was right next to him. "This is fun!"

"Do you have another peppermint?" Sidi asked Moussa. "Are we ready to head back to solid ground?"

Once you have been out on a boat looking back at where you live, everything seems changed. The blue water, the sea stretching, everything altered. Now the sea is a real place that can hold you. You will always know you might be elsewhere instead of on solid earth. You're not tied to the ground.

Aref had once floated with his dad on a

friend's sailboat and they came home that night feeling lighter and airy inside. Would flying feel this way too? Looking down on earth from high in the sky—would everything change even more, once you landed? Would standing on a shore in Michigan, or drifting out in a boat on any great lake let you feel connected to all the floating people of the world?

"Let's check the net for sardines," said Moussa, "before we head back in. We didn't quite get to their favorite spot, but just in case. . . ."

Hand over hand, he and Sidi pulled the heavy net into the boat. A large clump of seaweed was snagged in it, and a few tiny sardines.

Moussa shook his head. "Not very successful!"

"But look what I see," said Sidi, pointing. "A prize! A relic from the deep!"

It was an odd lumpy gray stone that looked a little like a person sitting down, hunched over.

"It's for you!" Sidi said, handing it to Aref. "No fish, but a sitting stone! I think it looks like me in the boat."

Aref laughed. "It does look like you. Does it get a face?"

"No, this one will remain pure, unblemished by human touch. But ask what it knows, listen closely, and guard the answer." Sidi handed it to Aref like a prize. Aref slipped the sitting stone into his pocket. A relic from the underworld. Frozen in time.

Boat Trip

Boat Trip
1. I caught two fish.
2. Sidi is not like Sinbad the Sailor. Sidi had to take a Tums.

Stretched-Out Day

That afternoon, Aref and Sidi made popcorn and watched a movie on TV about penguins. Then they decided to take naps. Sidi thought of it, but Aref agreed without saying anything. "The sea makes people sleepy," Sidi said, yawning. "This will be good for us. We can play games longer this evening. We can stay up late and have a stretched-out day."

Lying on the couch, his head on a red pillow,

Aref kept thinking that no matter what you say, there is something more inside that you can't say. You talk around it in a circle, like stirring water with a stick, when ripples swirl out from the center. You say something that isn't quite right and that's worse. Then you want to say, sorry! But no one knows what you mean.

He wished he could tell Sidi, you are the king of my heart forever, I don't care who else I meet, I don't care about traveling and new friends and different flavored yogurts, I only care about how nice you are and how much I cannot stand the thought of being far from you, ever, ever, ever.

But he could never say this.

Aref took the sitting stone out of his pocket because it was lumpy and placed it on the table next to him. It really sat up. Aref's body felt as if it was still bobbing in the boat. Then he fell asleep.

When they rose again after an hour, they both felt energized. "I dreamed of the boat!" Sidi said.

"So did I!"

"I was still on it."

"So was I."

"Let's get moving."

Sidi swept the floor and Aref washed the dishes. Then Sidi gave Aref all the 5 and 10 and 25 *baisa* coins from the kitchen table drawer. He dropped them into a green velvet pouch and said, "Show your new friends in the United States what our coins look like. Maybe you can trade some. I could give you a few interesting postage stamps too. Would you like that?"

"Yes," said Aref, knowing that Sidi's gifts would be hard to trade or give away.

That night, they climbed up to the roof to watch the moon rise over the sea. It was orange and full, like a big fat juicy melon. So quickly, the steaming air of the day cooled off and the world became softer. A breeze rose up around them. Someone far away was calling out, repeating echoing words they couldn't understand.

A bird flew over, so large and so fast Aref wondered if it might be a falcon. Sidi thought it was a vulture headed toward a dead rat down by the dock.

A plane took off from the airport and flew low over the city, at an angle. "Where do you think that one is going?" Aref asked.

"Maybe Teheran. Or Karachi. It's not the

biggest one and the biggest one that goes to Kuwait also goes to London or Germany."

How did Sidi know so many things?

"When you go to the airport in a few days," said Sidi, "I'll come straight home after dropping you and your mother, and climb to this roof and look up. And you look down, too. Promise me?"

His voice sounded thick now.

Aref, like swirling water, couldn't say anything.

Back downstairs, Sidi lit the old kerosene lamp he kept on his table. They played cards. Sidi could snap and shuffle cards much faster than Aref's parents could. They worked on the giant turtle puzzle that they obviously weren't going to be able to finish now—and only accomplished one corner of water. "What is the use of a puzzle anyway?" Aref asked.

"Patience," said Sidi. "The use of a puzzle is patience."

"I hate patience."

"No, you don't. It's the best talent we have."

Aref poured the dominoes out of their wooden box and he and Sidi dove into a game, playing twelve or fourteen times in a row, clicking the dominoes on the low marble-topped coffee table. And they tied. They always tied, winning the same number of games each before quitting. The kerosene light from the lamp danced on the walls. Sidi leaned back on the couch. "How often does it happen?" he asked. "Two champions in the same family!"

Sidi told Aref a few stories about when he was a boy, when none of the roads were paved and no tourists came and people still had donkeys and horses nuzzling around their houses and yards. Bread sellers and tea sellers would ride on the small dirt roads, calling out special bread and tea songs. "*Hoobz* for the people! *Shai* turned on high!" There were many camels in a caravan then, loaded with pots and pans and cloth and seeds and drums and threads and fruits and dates and tools. People were dependent on them.

"You definitely would have liked cooking outdoors all the time on those big flaming fire pits with huge pots suspended over them," Sidi said.

"Where did those fire pits go?"

"I don't know. We could look for them

264

someday. Maybe the earth swallowed them. We had one right outside in the backyard where the mint is now—you know how the mint is growing in a circle? I think it's growing in the ashes of the old fire pit."

Sidi closed his eyes and tipped his head to one side. "When I was young, I rode a galloping brown horse all the way to the turtle beach, which is very far, as you know, to see the turtles at night, slipping out of the sea . . . I even slept there."

"I want to do that," Aref said. "You know I do! Why have we never done that?" It sounded even better than just camping with other kids on the school field trip.

"We'll do it when you get back," Sidi promised. "I mean, we won't ride horses there, sorry, but we'll see if we can get a permit to camp there. We'll also drive south to Sana'a, Yemen, to see the fabulous ancient brown and white buildings with zigzags and polka dots, the most amazing buildings in the world, and we'll drive to Saudi Arabia to see towers and palaces and maybe we'll even go to Dubai to purchase little gold bricks from the mall machines, since you'll be bringing your big sack of American coins back here and need to invest them, and maybe we'll even sail to India, across that rough water, if we get very very brave. I don't know if I could take it, though. Too much boating might finish me off."

Aref laughed. "I'm sorry you felt sick, Sidi!"

"It's fine now. I took a Tums. I have recovered."

"We can just fly to India."

"By then you'll be an expert on flying. I have one more small surprise," Sidi said. "Are you tired again? I hope so. Because tonight . . . would you like to sleep on the roof?"

Open Air

Two bedrolls of blankets and quilts were waiting on the wooden shelf inside Sidi's clothes cupboard.

"Excellent!" said Aref.

"Can you blow out the lamp, please?" asked Sidi.

They lugged the bedrolls, along with a bed pillow for Sidi and a red velvety couch pillow for Aref, up the skinny stairs to the flat roof. Sidi unrolled a plastic tarp, then Aref smoothed out the quilts.

A rooster crowed from somewhere. Aref leaned over the edge of the roof to see if he could spot him. But the rooster was invisible in the dark.

"Is he confused?" asked Aref.

"He always does that," said Sidi. "He needs a new clock."

They looked out across the old portion of the city. "In my eyes I have a map of these lights," Sidi said.

"You do?"

"You can have one too. Just soak it all up and close your eyes, then look again till it is written in your brain."

They were quiet. A fire engine streaked across the map, down toward the shore, wailing loudly. "I don't want a fire engine in my brain," Aref said.

"Erase it. Let it pass, then look again."

They stood a few more moments in silence.

"I have it now," said Aref. A moon was at the top of his map and a breeze rattled the corner.

Sidi had a hard time squatting down on the ground to stretch out on his covers. "I haven't done this in a long time," he said, huffing. "Ouch! It would be better if we had two little mattresses. Sorry! I should have thought of that."

"I don't need a mattress," said Aref.

"You are a young pup!"

Aref kicked off his shoes and peeled off his socks. Sometimes it was fun to sleep in your clothes. "I am not a pup. Sidi, did you hear about the oldest gorilla in the world having a birthday this month? He is fifty-two and he has twelve children."

"Where did you hear this?"

"From Lena at school—she likes gorillas as much as I like turtles."

"Where does that gorilla live?"

"She didn't tell me."

"Let's be glad he's not having his birthday party on this roof."

They laughed. Then they laughed more.

Thick blackness salted with stars made a wide ceiling above them, even here, in the city. "Sidi, the sky is so huge," said Aref.

Sidi said, "I'm falling into it. Are you?"

They talked softly, whispering together, as if they didn't want to break a spell. They felt like birds wrapped in their own wings or suspended in the moving waves, comfortably gliding, or secret stones buried in hot sand for hundreds of years. They felt like part of the sky and everything under it. They were very tiny and they were also specks of dust floating in moonbeams and they could time-travel and be in more than one place at the same moment, and Sidi said in some ways he would always be a little boy too even though he didn't look like it anymore, and Aref said, "Sidi, I am also older than you." And all of this made sense to them.

Aref dreamed he was flying without an airplane. Sidi dreamed about the rooster speaking through a translator.

They woke up at the same time and told their dreams.

In the middle of the night, Sidi had said,

"Aref, I'm going to miss you terribly, you do know that?"

Aref felt warmed to hear this and sad, at the same time. He knew Sidi always tried to keep everything positive, so this was a rare comment from his happy tongue.

Contagious

Back at home, Mr. Al-Jundi from down the street showed up with his wife and seven children to say a dramatic good-bye to Aref and his mother. At least five of the children were coughing and sneezing. After they left, Aref's mom opened the windows to air out the rooms. She had tried to keep her scarf in front of her face while they were all standing there. "They seemed very contagious! We don't want to get colds before we go," she said.

Aref didn't like colds either, but he liked the word *contagious*. And he added it to his favorite word list. Maybe everything was contagious. His mom had always told him whining was contagious—he was old enough now to feel it might be true. Still, he did it sometimes. You couldn't help it. Complaining was contagious and also a little delicious.

Different Kinds of Contagious
1. If one person likes a song and keeps singing it, it gets stuck in your head.
2. If one person wears rainbow colored shoelaces, everyone wants them.

3. If one kid at lunchtime says the spinach in the school cafeteria tastes rotten, everyone might think so.

Maybe if your friends saw the stones you had collected, or your grandfather had given to you, they thought about collecting them too. Maybe it was all up to you. To everybody, every single day. What you did, what you said . . . could change what happened. Or how everyone felt.

"We will win this game." Aref knew that's what some soccer players said before every game. Even if they were smaller and younger, even if they knew both teams couldn't win, the players said it, to pump up their own bravery. "We will win. We will be brave. We will pass this test. We will stand on the stage and sing a solo without croaking like a toad."

Aref was turning around inside his own mind. That's what it felt like. He was standing inside the doorway of his still-jumbled bedroom, staring at it. What a nice room. *See you again someday. Be nice to my cousins.* Maybe he could make a little space for bravery inside his fear, maybe just a little. Maybe it would grow. Maybe sleeping on a roof had done something to him.

In his notebook he wrote,

Breaking News
1. The Al-Jundi family was sneezing a lot, now our house might be polluted.
2. Sleeping on the roof is really

the best thing. If you have a
flat roof, you should try it. But
if you don't have a flat roof you
will ROLLLLLLLL off.
3. Mom has only one more meeting
at work tomorrow, then she will be
FINISHED so she is in a good mood.

"We received three more messages from
your father!" said his mom, pointing at the
computer, open on the table. Now his dad was
writing in all CAPS. There were ARABIC
RESTAURANTS WITH HOT FRESHLY
BAKED BREAD, EVEN IN MICHIGAN.
There were CONCERTS OF ARABIC MUSIC.
You could walk down the street and hear
TEN DIFFERENT LANGUAGES BEING
SPOKEN—JUST LIKE IN MUSCAT. WENT

TO GREAT CHINESE RESTAURANT TODAY. WE CAN EAT MEXICAN BREAKFAST TACOS ON CORNER WHEN YOU COME. LOOKING FORWARD TO YOUR ARRIVAL!!! In a special note to Aref, he said, OUR APARTMENT BUILDING ALLOWS CATS AND DOGS. MAYBE WE CAN GET AN AMERICAN CAT FROM THE HUMANE SOCIETY AND NAME IT MISH-MISH TWO.

Aref wrote back, "YES TO CAT!!!!"

With only two days before leaving, the telephone seemed to be ringing constantly. Aref's mom kept saying, "Good-bye! Thanks for calling! We will miss you too!" to everyone. People Aref had never seen before were stopping by the house and ringing the bell. Some of his mom's students brought her a little travel kit packed with Omani lotions that smelled lemony and a silver necklace.

Miss Rose, the secretary from the English department at Muscat University, brought them a big floppy red geranium plant in a pink clay pot and his mom thanked her, but when Miss Rose left, his mom said, "What? Does she think I can carry a plant to America?"

They would leave the geranium by their front door for Hani and Shadi to water.

World Traveler Leaves Friendly Note in Empty Closet

When Sidi showed up in the middle of their last afternoon at home with fresh hot pita bread from the bakery, the house smelled instantly delicious. "You all need some energy over here," he said. "I don't think you're going to the bakery anymore, so I went one last time for you."

Aref pulled off a triangular piece of warm

bread and stuffed it into his mouth. His mother cut up their very last chunk of salty white cheese.

"I think we forgot to have lunch," she said. They filled some bread with pitted dates and cheese. It was the best meal in the world.

"I'm here to work!" Sidi announced when they were all full. "What do you need done?"

"Can you get our slowpoke to finish packing his suitcase, please?" asked Aref's mother. "No more delays! He needs to pick his very favorite clothes, and whatever he wants that fits into that suitcase, today, absolutely today! All other things will have to be packed into our last open boxes and stored. That room must be completely empty except for furniture when we leave."

Aref closed his eyes and pinched up his cheeks.

"Let's go! I'll help you if you help yourself," said Sidi as they climbed the stairs to his room. "You take all the shirts and pants out of your closet and drawers and pile them on the bed. No more playing around."

Aref loaded his arms with hangers and clothes and threw them on the bed, falling on top of them.

"Perfect!" said Sidi. "Now I'll hold each one up and you say yes or no."

He held up a yellow shirt.

Aref said, "No!"

He held up a green shirt with one wide white stripe around the middle.

"No!"

"Come on now, sailor-boy, are you going to

go naked in Michigan? You have to say YES sometimes or your mom will make all the decisions and you don't want that to happen, right?"

So Aref said yes to a navy blue shirt and a black shirt with a yellow sun and OMAN on it. He said yes to a maroon sweatshirt, blue shorts, long pants with cuffs, a brown sweater, and blue jeans. Mish-Mish was sitting in the corner of the room watching them. "Do you think she knows?" Aref asked.

"Yes. But she is . . . patient. She will wait for you, as I will."

Together they folded underpants and white T-shirts.

"Let's get this job done, then go out and have ice cream," said Sidi. "Good idea? You like black socks? Sports socks? Why do you have a thousand socks?"

Sidi was folding the last pair of blue jeans now. "See, it doesn't take long at all. These look a little small," he said, holding them up. "Would you like to leave these here?"

"YES! Throw them away! Tell me the story about the big pan and the little pan. The talking donkey. The monkey with a hat on his bottom!" Aref knew the big pan would be the mother of the little pan. The donkey would say, "Slow down, human race." The monkey would ask, "Who told you a hat has to go on a head?"

"You know them all," said Sidi. "You will carry the stories in here." He held up Aref's small feather pillow. "Tuck this into your suitcase right this minute. Remember when you got it? Of course you don't, you were just a baby. But I brought it to you. Every time you sleep, my stories will be in there whispering. Now tell me one thing—will you still be a big eater when you come back?"

"For sure. A big talker and a big eater. Maybe even a bigger eater. Or, a faster one."

"You will also be tall and a world traveler. The boy who saw another country and came home again. The boy who saw snow."

Now they had the books to deal with. It was horrible to leave books behind.

"I'd just keep them right here on the shelves for your cousins to enjoy. You know, you can start fresh with new books when you get to America," Sidi suggested. "They have plenty of books there. Get a library card, go to the library, check out new books every week, like you do here. Maybe you shouldn't take any of these."

"No, I have to," Aref said. He grabbed the two new books he had been saving to read on the plane. One was about Egyptian relics and tombs and pharoahs and the other was the diary of a couple of friends who rode bicycles across America, having adventures all the way.

"You know what I thought of?" said Sidi. "You could write a welcome note to Hani and Shadi and tape it inside the closet on the wall."

Aref paused before answering. "You think? Would they like that?"

"Sure, they would. Who wouldn't? Wouldn't you like to find a friendly note taped inside your new closet in Michigan?"

So Aref found one last piece of orange

construction paper and wrote in dark blue marker: "*Ahlan!* Welcome to the cool cave room! I hope you will be very nice to Mish-Mish. Pet her a lot and she will be happy. Be careful, she scratches if she's mad. Have fun living here! Send me some e-mails! LOVE, AREF."

He drew a big star at the top and made swooshing marks so the star looked as if it were flying across the sky. He taped his note to the wall inside the closet.

"They will like it," Aref said.

Sidi laughed. "See, that's the spirit!"

"Hey, happy people, I made you something you love downstairs," Mom called.

They could smell it. She'd been stirring rice and milk and cinnamon in a big pot, making rice pudding, their favorite dessert.

They liked it even more than ice cream. Aref sniffed the cinnamon and knew his house was smiling.

"Guess what?" Aref's mother said. "I just finished the bag of cinnamon. That means it's almost time to leave!"

The Rule of Muscat

Sidi took the last small piece of white paper still sitting on Aref's desk and wrote something on it, closed his eyes and wrote some more, then folded the paper up very tiny and tucked it into the inside pocket of Aref's suitcase. "This says I will visit Mish-Mish with special cat treats when you are gone, and I will be waiting for the telephone to ring every Sunday when you and your parents call to tell me what is going on. Also, there are some secret messages on it."

Aref reached toward the suitcase pocket. He wanted to unfold it now.

"No!" Sidi tapped his hand back. "You can't look at it till you get there. It is the rule of Muscat." Then he took some stones Aref couldn't see from his pocket, kissed them, and slipped them into the pouch where the note was. He clapped his hands and smiled.

Strange Animal

Aref and Sidi were sitting outside on the peaceful back patio for the last time, the evening before Aref and his mother left for the United States. Empty bowls from their rice pudding rested close together on the table. They had each eaten two full bowls. Silver spoons leaned in the bowls like little spoon-flags. The warm wind smelled of vanilla and cinnamon, same as the pudding. Sometimes you felt exactly where you were, and nowhere else.

Aref pressed the buttons on a remote control that made his little zombie-man with glistening red eyes walk across the table.

"What is that thing?" asked Sidi.

"It's a zombie."

"I don't like it," Sidi said. "It scares me. Put him to bed."

Aref laughed. "You're so silly, Sidi! He's nice. He's a nice zombie."

"Love is a strange animal," Sidi said, out of the blue. This was odd.

"What do you mean? What kind of animal?" Aref asked.

"I'm not sure. What do you think?"

Aref said, "A wolf?"

"Maybe a wolf. But no, we don't see the wolf

often enough. The wolf is hiding. Keeping his big teeth to himself. Maybe a butterfly?"

"Why?" asked Aref.

"Oh, the surprise of them. The beauty. We feel cheered when we see one."

Aref's mother adored butterflies—she knew their names and geometric markings. Sometimes they fluttered over the patio in a crowd. His mother had planted bushes with purple flowers that they liked to drink from. Aref had gone on many butterfly-viewing expeditions with her and wrote his last science paper about them, so he knew a lot too. His notebook was filled with butterfly data.

Butterflies
1. Butterflies follow their own schedules.

2. They fly somewhere and land briefly, then disappear quickly. Sometimes they migrate in large flocks, even thousands.

3. Oman has the "fig blue" and the rare "swallowtail" and the common "blue pansy."

4. The "Asian grass blue" in the north of Oman can disguise itself—as grass.

5. The lime butterfly has a very large wingspan and gobbles up all the leaves of the lime trees, its favorite food. Lime trees wish they would go far, far away to another place and stay there.

6. Actually there are 53 different species of butterflies in Oman which are too many to talk about right now.

"Sidi, do you think there are butterflies in Michigan?"

"I'm sure of it," Sidi said. "They'll be fluttering around, just wait. We've had a whole week of fluttering around, did you notice?"

"It was great. I liked every single day. And you know what, butterflies are not fragile. That's what Mom says. They might look fragile, but they can migrate hundreds of miles without an airplane."

"Like a turtle, right. Or even like those cranes we didn't see by the pond," said Sidi.

"But we saw their nests. Right."

"It's popular," said Sidi. "A popular activity. Going away and coming back."

When you stared hard at the dirt of the ground and the grasses and the mint right before dark, you could feel it all breathing. It was the softest time in the whole day. Sidi took a deep breath too.

"Maybe love is all the animals mixed together," said Sidi. The zombie had fallen over onto the ground and Aref let him lie there, buzzing. "That makes sense." He put out his hand and patted Aref's hand.

"Yes," said Aref. "And love is a zombie too." A green lizard had crawled up onto the zombie and was staring at it.

"Let's let his battery run out," said Sidi.

"No!" Aref leaned over and rescued the

zombie, flipping the switch that turned off his light. The lizard scampered away. "I'm sticking him in my suitcase."

"Excellent. Now I can relax," said Sidi.

Beyond them the lights of Muscat glittered under a pink sky that stretched all the way down to the water's edge. Aref imagined a fisherman folding his net. A fish no one could see was smiling.

And the secret rule of Muscat? Aref would keep it under the stone with a face that no one had noticed in a hundred years, in his Michigan windowsill, lined up with other stones Sidi had given him. It would say, "Dear Aref, don't forget everything you love about your country is buried safely in the sand at our beach. Eggs hatching soon."

Aref stood up, stacked the four bowls, with

the two spoons balanced in the top one, then walked like a slow and dignified person into the kitchen. "Hey, Mom!" he said. "I know you won't believe this, but—I'm packed."